Courtyard Corpse

A Cassie Hall Mystery

by
Sherry Lodge

For information, email **Cozy Cat Press**, cozycatpress@aol.com or visit our website at: www.cozycatpress.com

COZY CAT
P R E S S

ISBN: 978-1-946063-13-7

Printed in the United States of America

Cover design by Paula Ellenberger
www.paulaellenberger.com

1 2 3 4 5 6 7 8 9 10

Dedicated to Cassie Hall's fans

CHAPTER 1

New resident Bunny Ace was trapped between a dolly stacked with cardboard boxes and me—Cassie Hall, the daytime concierge—as we rode in the elevator to the Parkstone's 12th floor. I leaned against the elevator wall to make myself as unremarkable as possible while Bunny fidgeted with her wedding ring as if there were a slew of other places she'd rather be.

"Cassie, we wanted the freight elevator, not the regular elevator, correct?" Bunny said, surveying the boxes. "Now you see why."

I held onto Jet-Setter, one of the building cats, to keep him, unsuccessfully, from scratching the boxes as Bunny looked at him sternly. The problem was Bunny Ace was all business, and Jet-Setter was all boxes. Then, to my relief, Jet-Setter leapt to the floor. Bunny ignored the fur ball, and continued, "Do you mind fixing the reservation?"

"Of course not," I said as the elevator stopped on the 12th floor, and I quickly pressed the red button as the movers cleared the boxes and Jet-Setter scampered out.

Bunny continued, "And if it's not too much trouble, I'd like to ask you to turn up the air conditioning in the building." She paused. "I'd hate to see Kip break a sweat."

Kip Ace was a professional golfer and Bunny's husband whose handsome looks and net worth made me tremble. If Bunny didn't want Kip to break a sweat, then I'd do my best to make sure that didn't happen. This was the Parkstone, after all, and the residents' quality of life was of the utmost importance. "Once I'm back at the concierge desk, I'll fix everything right away."

With a bejeweled finger, Bunny motioned for me to press the lobby button. "Let's go there now, shall we?"

Kip Ace stood in front of the concierge desk wearing a smile as long as the Parkstone's lush courtyard. I was still in awe that my childhood golf idol was standing right in front of me. I couldn't help asking for his autograph, and he did one better, signing a Parkstone brochure with the phrase: *Stay out of life's bunkers*. I then placed the brochure between the computer and my name placard on the concierge desk. It was better than any amenity at the Parkstone.

"Are you from the area?" Bunny asked, having mentioned earlier that she and Kip were Bethesda natives.

I wondered what lurked behind her question. "I'm from Cherry Creek, Colorado," I said.

Bunny looked at me quizzically. "What brought you halfway across the country?"

"My boyfriend," I said, not wanting to say much more. She looked at me blankly. I continued, "He's a Maryland homicide detective."

"A homicide detective?" she said loudly, placing a hand over her chest. People were always shocked to find out Eric's profession. I continued, "I moved for him once he got the job, and I'm really happy I did."

She slightly rolled her eyes. "Well, everyone's happy once they've moved to Bethesda—even I will be, right, Kip?"

"Right, dear," Kip said as he milled around the lobby looking at the Chihuly sculpture with feigned interest. Deep down I knew the answer I'd given Bunny was only half the truth. The other half was buried deep like a squirrel's acorns in the courtyard during wintertime.

She eyed me. "That seems like a long way to uproot oneself for a boyfriend," she said. "Without a ring on your finger?" She paused, turning around to look at Kip. "Although nowadays, who knows."

I smiled politely. The ring issue was another sore spot. For fifteen long years, I'd been hoping Eric would propose. And as much as it was my job to be there for residents, I was hoping this conversation would end soon. Sometimes the day-to-day interactions at the Parkstone could be trying.

As Kip walked up to the concierge desk, I welcomed the distraction.

"Do you have cuff links?" he said raising an eyebrow.

I smiled. "I don't, but the building might." A rummage through the desk drawers produced two options: "Teal colored tie knots or gold swivel bars?"

"The tie knots, my darling," he said. "My own are packed away in the depths of those boxes. And Bunny and I have a black-tie gala to attend."

I was enamored. Kip Ace was the only person who'd ever called me *darling*, and the only person I knew who actually wore cuff links and attended black-tie events. As far as I was concerned, Bunny was a lucky woman, but she seemed more on edge than Kip about the move and downsizing. The only reason they'd moved to the Parkstone in the first place was because their mansion had been struck by lightning. What could be worse luck that that? And Bunny's best friend Ginnie Langford had lived at the Parkstone for years, so the Aces said it seemed like as good a place as any.

In droves, the movers brought boxes up to the Aces' new 12th floor apartment. Boxes marked "Kip's Sweaters," "Bunny's Trinkets" and "Last Season's

Gucci." Everything was well until Bunny almost had a coughing fit when one of the movers dropped a box marked "Swarovski" on the lobby floor.

The bad luck continued.

At least I could make some things right for them. I changed the elevator reservation to the freight elevator for Bunny and made the temperature cooler for Kip. Then Bunny said, "Can you get Lillian, the leasing agent, to answer some last-minute questions?" I was quickly logging off the computer when Bunny said, "Well, *can* you?"

Her bitter tone struck a chord, momentarily breaking my tough customer service shell, an exterior I'd built up from two years of working at the Parkstone. To make matters worse, she said it in front of Kip, which made me turn a shade of crabapple red.

From then on it became a game of Cassandra and Bunny.

A little more than a year later and Bunny was still barking orders, but I was a lot slower to resolve her complaints. One morning, after Bunny's second phone call to the concierge desk, I decided to wait to pick it up until the last ring. "Parkstone Concierge Desk, Cassie Hall speaking," I said as officially as I could. "How may I help you?"

"Bunny, here," she said as quickly as if she'd just thrown a dart. "The peach peplum or the red peplum shirt with the black skirt." There was a pause. "For brunch. Kip and I have been so busy as of late that this is one of our first jaunts together in a while and I want it to be perfect. So, Cassie, what pair do you think would go together better?"

"Without seeing it, I'd think a peach peplum shirt would go better with a black skirt."

"That's what I thought, too, Cassie. Just wanted a second opinion."

"Happy to help," I said secretly liking that I was one of the Parkstone's go-to fashionistas. "Is there anything else I can help with today?"

"No, Cassie, that's all," she said. "Now hopefully it'll fit."

She laughed nervously. I was happy for Kip and Bunny, and I was sure Bunny would look dashing in the outfit I'd helped choose.

I hung up the phone, which had been ringing off the hook, as I fielded resident calls about the water being shut off. I hadn't had time to do the morning rounds. I was also a little late that morning, which I knew my boss Royce Baxter would not be happy about. Half an hour later, after answering more phone calls, I began to gather my coat to make my rounds.

The Parkstone building was shaped like a donut, so the private crabapple tree courtyard in the center was secure and remained exclusive to residents. The main courtyard happenings included residents sun-tanning, watching the moon, or having a picnic. In fact, the luxury of the courtyard was what had enticed the Aces to sign on the dotted line in the first place. Besides the fact that Bunny's best friend Ginnie lived at the Parkstone. Bunny liked sunbathing near the crabapple trees, and Kip cherished practicing his golf swing.

All of a sudden, from behind my perch at the concierge desk, I heard a loud scream coming from the courtyard. A dark shadow flittered among the crabapple trees. I grabbed the vintage key from my Lily Pulitzer dress pocket and headed outside. It was cool and crisp and there was a chilling breeze. I opened the large wrought iron gate, which closed with a loud thud behind me.

The lawn smelled of freshly cut grass, strewn about the cascading hills, which looked grandiose. The topiary was perfectly clipped into shapes of elephants and tiered trees, which loomed above.

I began walking along the row of crabapple trees and noted that nothing was out of place. The stone benches were in place; the large sunflowers were casting shadows on the grass and it was quieter than the lobby on a Sunday morning. Where had that scream come from? I continued under the dark shade of the trees, when just above the hill, I spotted unidentified shapes sticking out of the grass.

Was something lurking in the shadows?

I headed along the crabapple trees that hugged the brick path—Jet-Setter and Cashmere, the Parkstone cats, in tow.

The shapes were shifting with the moving shadows. I began to pick up speed as my heart beat faster than a resident's furious dings of the concierge bell. Something in the courtyard was askew. I picked up Cashmere and held her tight.

I squinted to get a better look up the hill. There was a shape I could make out. It was shoes. And not just any shoes. They were fancy dress shoes! I continued up the hill cautiously. Jet-Setter darted in front, pawing at fallen crabapples that were scattered and smooshed on the grass.

From the top of the hill in the sunlight, I could see what was in the shadows: the slumped body of a large man. He was wearing almond-colored plaid golf shorts and a fancy tweed blazer and a "Fore the Cure" t-shirt I'd designed for tomorrow's off-site afternoon charity golf tournament. He was also wearing a Fitbit on his right wrist that caught the glare of the sun. Bunny was going to be furious. It was Kip Ace.

"Mr. Ace?" I whispered. Had someone been fighting with Kip? "Mr. Ace," I said again.

He didn't move. I looked at Kip's body. There were grass stains on his shirt. Had there been an altercation? His unmoving body was becoming more haunting by the minute.

Jet-Setter pawed at the grass near Kip's body and I scooped him up before he could sneak any closer.

"Kiiip?" I said, my voice quivering. I put Cashmere and Jet-Setter down to check Kip's neck for a pulse. Looking at Kip's motionless body, my mind drifted to the other reason I'd decided to move to Bethesda: my high school friend, Hunter Appleby, who'd died in a hit-and-run crash our senior year—the mystery still unsolved.

Like it was yesterday, images fluttered through my mind of Hunter lying on the four-lane street after the collision as a car blur zipped away and others screeched to a halt. My tense stomach hurt and I began tearing up. Then I shut my eyes sharply. *Focus, for Kip's sake.* I fumbled for Kip's wrist and checked his pulse. There was none. This marked two dead bodies I'd hovered over hoping for a pulse. And both times I hadn't gotten what I wanted. I picked up the cats again.

"Kiiip?" I managed to say. No response. A dried crabapple-colored stain coated the back of his straw-colored hair. How could something like this happen to Kip? Stillness crept in as the sun continued to fill the courtyard.

I checked his pulse again. His still body haunted me. I thought I'd give it another try and maybe the outcome would be different. But it wasn't. I couldn't believe what was right in front of me: Kip Ace was dead cold on that crisp October morning.

CHAPTER 2

I screamed louder than I'd ever screamed in my 35 years of living. When had he died? Was it moments before I found him or last night, when the night shift concierge was on duty? It mattered to me, and it was going to matter to Royce Baxter of Baxter Enterprises, who owned the Parkstone along with many other luxury apartment buildings in the Washington D.C. area. He was as rigid as a lease agreement.

I didn't want to be as shallow as others perceived me to be and think only of myself at this moment, but if Kip had died on my watch, I might get fired. And if so, I'd surely lose my apartment at the Parkstone and life as I knew it would change. I knew I wasn't heading back to Cherry Creek, Colorado.

There was no way I could afford my studio apartment in the heart of Bethesda, Maryland, without my concierge discount. Even if I saved all the money I'd made from my concierge job and side design and fashion gigs. Bethesda living was just too expensive.

I'd already been late to work one too many times, and building management could easily find a way to find me at fault for Kip's death. I hadn't made rounds of the courtyard that morning, and if I'd done so, Kip Ace might still be alive. I shuddered at the thought that this was somehow my fault.

I looked down at Mr. Ace's body and screamed again.

This was madness. Was no one around? On the back of his head, the crabapple-colored stain looked like it was a large gash, as if he'd been hit with a blunt object. Kip hadn't just died, he'd been murdered!

Who would kill the affable Kip? He was the nicest man in the building. Not to mention the most successful, with a net worth of more than $15 million.

Maybe someone was jealous of his success?

I had the urge to check his pulse again, just to see if maybe my screams had startled him into being. No such luck.

And no one was responding to my screams. It was as if my screams had fallen into the vast void of the courtyard, which seemed larger than ever. I decided to get out my cellphone and dial 911.

My hands—with now appropriately ghoulish black nail polish—trembled as I dialed the number.

Just then, Mrs. Canterbury appeared on the scene. "Hellllooooooo? My dear, what's wrong?" she said. "I heard screaming."

Mrs. Canterbury was an NIH scientist. She was brilliant. The Parkstone was home to some of the brightest, most fascinating people in Bethesda: Nobel Laureates, Ivy League graduates, athletes, scientists and programmers. All living under one very expensive stone roof.

She looked down at Mr. Ace and gasped. She grabbed her chest as if she was having trouble breathing. "Good God! Is he—?"

"Mrs. Canterbury, please contain yourself," I said, "I'm on the phone with 911."

"He's dead!" she wailed.

"Mrs. Canterbury," I said, "Please! Let's wait for…" Then a voice came on the other line. "911? Yes, I'd like to report a murder."

"Murder?!?" Mrs. Canterbury said, fanning herself with an air fan. "Murder at the Parkstone! I can't believe it."

Mrs. Canterbury fainted and fell to the ground. Why was everyone keeling over during my shift? "Yes, 911, I'd like to report the murder of famous golfer Kip Ace. At the residence of the Parkstone. And a fainter. Mrs. Canterbury. Same address."

The man's voice on the other end was collected: "We'll send a few squad cars right over. Stay calm. Can you tell me what happened?"

Speaking quickly, I told the story of the recent events and how they'd unfolded. I kept checking on Mrs. Canterbury throughout the story as she was regaining her wits. The 911 operator promised me the squad car would be there in five minutes or less. And he was right. Sirens filled the air no more than a couple minutes later and I ran back through the building's lobby to greet the detectives.

They bustled through the Parkstone's revolving doors. "Detective Peters," said the first detective, giving me a firm handshake even though I already knew full well who he was. He was tall and handsome with biceps that looked noticeably sculpted in his suit and tie. He was the man I'd been dating for the past 15 years. He was the man who every time he dug his hand into his pocket I'd hope he was pulling out a ring.

"How are you doing?" he said, pulling me aside.

"Besides the dead resident in the courtyard and the one who fainted next to him? Just peachy."

"I got here as fast as I could," he said.

I believed him. Eric was reliable. He continued, "I couldn't believe it when I saw the address."

Then another detective came up to us. "I take it this is not a normal day at the Parkstone?" he said, eying the ornate marble interior. "Detective Williams," he said, shaking my hand. "Pleased to meet you."

The police did their thing and soon Eric was back to speak to me.

"Everything's going to be okay." He motioned towards Detective Williams. "I'll take it from here," Eric said. Then he turned back to me, placing his strong hands on my shoulders. "We're going to have to ask you and all of the residents a few questions. We're going to have to scour this place from top to bottom, I'm afraid. We're placing the Parkstone and its residents on lockdown effective immediately."

"Hold residents captive in the Parkstone? That's not going to go over well," I said, picturing all of the irate Parkstone inhabitants yelling at me nonetheless.

Detective Williams eyed the posh lobby some more. "There are worse places to be holed up."

I thought about the training manual I'd received my first day on the job that contained an emergency section which stated that the building and its residents should not be on lockdown for more than 24 hours for any reason, murder included.

I thought this would be a good time to mention that, before things got out of control. As if they hadn't already. "According to building policy, the building can't be on lockdown for more than 24 hours," I said. "I can get the manual to prove it."

Eric shook his head. "Police procedure trumps your manual in the case of murder, Ms. Hall. So, we can start with a 24-hour lockdown, but if it needs to be extended for any reason we can make that happen, too."

Why was he calling me Ms. Hall? My relief that the detective I'd been dating for years was here at my side, was somehow squelched by his formality.

Two could play that game. "The policy manual is intended to make life here at the Parkstone more pleasant for residents," I said. "Parkstone owner Royce Baxter would attest to that."

"This is a Baxter building?" Williams said, still looking in awe at the interior. "That explains it, since they own most luxury buildings in Bethesda."

"And I work here," I said. "And I know he wouldn't want one of his buildings on lockdown longer than a day."

"The quicker we solve this case, the better," said Eric. "We'll place a mandatory lockdown of the building to be instituted immediately and to last 24 hours. Okay? That's in line with the Parkstone policy. Hopefully, we'll solve the case in that time frame, and maybe even sooner!"

Considering I'd been waiting for an engagement ring for 15 years, I knew that Eric and I had very different notions of the word "soon." "Yes, hopefully sooner than that," I said.

This was all so nerve-wrecking. Nothing like this had happened in any building I'd ever lived in, or worked at, and the Parkstone was the last place I'd suspect it.

Eric looked at me. "Ms. Hall—"

"Call me Cassie," I said. I had known him for nearly half my life. It only seemed natural.

"I'm on the job," he said. I raised an eyebrow. He continued, "Ms. Hall, your job right now is to alert all residents of this lockdown and shut all entrance and exit ways to the building. We'll also need a map of the building."

My head hurt just thinking of all the unhappy residents who couldn't go about their normal Saturday routine. I was going to get an earful about it from everyone. I found the Bose sound system behind the desk. *Here goes nothing.*

"Dear esteemed Parkstone residents. This is Cassie, your friendly front desk concierge. I regret to inform you there has been a murder in the building. For the safety of the residents, we request that you do not leave the building for the next 24 hours while the police investigate. This includes access to the courtyard. Thank you for your understanding in this matter."

I clicked off the sound system and braced for the onslaught of unhappy residents. I had spotted one already. It was Mary Chris Farley, whose long fishtail braid was swept along her shoulder. Her face looked paler than the marble floors, and was in stark contrast to her burgundy hair. She was pallid, as if she was haunted by something. I waved to try and break her cold, long stare, but she didn't flinch.

CHAPTER 3

Detective Williams walked over to the concierge desk tapping the bell repeatedly even though I was sitting right there. I used to laugh sometimes at the different ways people would ring the bell. Mr. Gillrot tapped the bell frantically, Rich Gibbons left long pauses between taps and Bunny would strike the bell once, with one long stinging, ding!

Detective Williams hunched his shoulders and put his hands around his waist. "We're going to need to ask you a few questions," he said, "seeing as how you discovered the body."

"I stumbled across it, yes," I said, hoping the questioning wasn't going to be too extensive, because there were residents to attend to. "And there's not much to tell. How you saw the body is how I found it. Kip was lying there face-planted into the grass."

"Did you notice anything suspicious?"

"Besides the dead body?" I said. "No. Not a thing. That was it. There was a golf club in his hand and holes like circle marks dotting the grass next to him. That seemed suspicious, but I don't know why. Just that I don't know what caused them."

I was the first person who found Kip dead. I didn't want them to think I was the last to see him alive.

Just then Mr. Gillrot, who strangely hadn't been downstairs to the lobby for his regular cup of morning coffee, appeared on the scene. "Twenty-four hour lockdown?" he shouted. "In this place? Over my—"

Then he stopped abruptly, probably thinking better of saying *over my dead body* seeing as the Parkstone was mourning the death of one of its residents.

He continued. "So who died? I watch this place like a hawk and didn't see anything suspicious the past couple of days."

It was true that Mr. Gillrot—the lobby barnacle—watched over the happenings of the Parkstone obsessively. "Mr. Ace has left us," I said. "He was found, by me, in the courtyard this morning."

"Well I'll be damned," he said in disbelief. "A likeable fellow like that found dead? That's quite shocking. Really quite shocking actually. Don't you think, Cassie?" He pondered for a moment. "So all of us here are *suspects*?" He looked up questioningly.

I nodded. "Please understand, Mr. Gillrot," I said with the full understanding that Mr. Gillrot would not understand.

He crossed his arms. "I don't. I really don't."

I exhaled deeply. This was going to be a long conversation. He continued, "What I understand all right is this: First Baxter Enterprises takes our money, charging us an exorbitant amount in rent—I mean mind boggling—and then we gotta be interrogated about a death we don't know anything about. Can you see why I'm frustrated?"

"Correct," I said, wondering when Mr. Gillrot would get the hang of this 24-hour lockdown.

"Well, I've gotta solution. Maybe I'll just stop paying rent. They say I can't leave. I say I can't pay my rent. That sounds fair."

When he put it that way, it sounded worse than I could have expected. Mr. Gillrot was going to revolt. He defiantly kept his arms crossed and leaned against the concierge desk as if he wasn't going anywhere anytime soon. And, because of the lockdown, he wasn't.

I cleared my throat. "The detectives will be by to interview all the suspects—I mean residents," I said catching my slip-up. Sometimes communicating with the residents didn't get any easier. "Just hold tight."

"Suspects?!" he said. "I thought Kip Ace was great! And I haven't been near the courtyard in days. Used to go there all the time to unwind and get my thoughts out. But this October has been so unforgiving. You can track my FOB activity if you'd like." There were no FOBs needed to access the courtyard, just a large wrought iron gate. He paused. "Wait until Mrs. Canterbury gets a load of this."

I gasped. Mrs. Canterbury!

I ran out to the courtyard to find Mrs. Canterbury sitting on the bricks on the side of the lawn. Mr. Gillrot arrived shortly after I did, huffing and puffing up the hill. Mrs. Canterbury had fainted when she'd discovered Mr. Ace had been murdered. And now she was sitting on the outskirts of the courtyard, flanked by paramedics and holding a cold compress to her head. How quickly things can change.

"I'm all right, I'm all right, please," she said. "Don't worry about me, please. Use your time to find out what happened to Mr. Ace."

Thank goodness she was coherent again, even though she still seemed dazed.

Mr. Gillrot—the know-it-all—wedged himself between the paramedics and Mrs. Canterbury. "Did you hear they're holding us hostage?"

"Mr. Gillrot, please!" I said, squeezing past him and the paramedics to speak to Mrs. Canterbury. She looked so frail sitting on the brick sidewalk. It was bad enough Mr. Gillrot had followed me out there, now he was exacerbating the situation. Mrs. Canterbury needed to rest. I put a hand on her shoulder. "There's a 24-hour period when the detectives will be investigating the crime. The residents are to stay in the Parkstone. Courtyard access is not permitted."

"What if we're expecting guests?" she said.

"Unfortunately, there are no guests allowed during this period," I said, hoping Mrs. Canterbury wasn't expecting anyone. She paused. "There's good news," I added.

"Oh, what's the good news dear?" Mrs. Canterbury said.

"We will be accepting mail and package deliveries," I said with a perky smile, hoping it would make up for all the other inconveniences.

Mr. Gillrot snarled. "Well that doesn't do us any good, now does it?" he shouted.

"Please, Mr. Gillrot," I said. "Mrs. Canterbury isn't feeling well."

"Maybe that's because she just learned the building is on lockdown, *and* no guests are allowed," he said. His wiry glasses made him seem even more persnickety. "What do you think about *that*?"

This caught the attention of the detectives who were mulling around the covered body. Their group dispersed and Detective Williams grabbed Mr. Gillrot by the arm. "You're coming with us," he said, escorting Mr. Gillrot back to the lobby and out of my hair for a while.

"How long did I faint?" Mrs. Canterbury said.

"Couldn't have been more than a few minutes," I said. "Long enough for Mr. Gillrot to run his mouth and ask where you were. I'm sorry he was so disruptive."

She moved the cold compress to the other side of her forehead. "I really do hope they find out what happened to Mr. Ace. He was such a sweet man. Loved golf, his wife, and his wines," she said with a smile. "Rumor had it he liked Ginnie, too."

Was Mrs. Canterbury still a little bit out of it? It sounded as if she was suggesting that Mr. Ace liked resident Ginnie Langford, his wife Bunny's best friend. That didn't seem to make sense at all.

I did know that Kip liked wine though. As Mrs. Canterbury said, it was true that Kip had an extensive wine collection in the Parkstone's penthouse wine cellar. I remembered the day he and Bunny moved in, an entire temperature-controlled U-Haul had arrived, dedicated to aged and expensive chardonnays and Bordeauxs that were now in the Parkstone wine cellar.

"The detectives are working as diligently as possible on the case," I said. "It's best now that you take care of yourself and get back to 100 percent health."

"I work at the NIH, the nation's premiere health institute. Surely, they'll let me leave to go there now, don't you think?" she said with a hopeful smirk.

"Rules are rules, and Mr. Baxter would be very clear about this one because it's for the safety of the residents," I said, which reminded me I'd have to inform the Baxter headquarters of what had happened.

"Safety of the residents? Well, it isn't very safe to have us locked up here with a killer, now is it?" Mrs. Canterbury said, steadying herself on the edge of the lawn.

The residents were really good at arguing. They would not make it easy for the detectives.

The paramedics helped Mrs. Canterbury up and back to her apartment. How would the detectives be able to solve this mystery in 24 hours without help? I knew I was as good a sleuth as any. Since Hunter's murder case in high school, finding the bad guy had always a prerogative of mine, especially because detectives never did close the case. Not that I thought Eric—now lead homicide detective on the case—couldn't solve the crime.

But this was personal. I'd been a huge fan of Kip's since I was young and remembered following him on tour, buying a copy of his book *Ace It*! and then about a year ago helping him and Bunny when they'd moved into the Parkstone, even though Bunny was up in arms about moving in. They'd already been run out of one home, and now—Kip was murdered!

I knew I should have been heading back to the lobby, but thought investigating the crime a bit couldn't hurt.

CHAPTER 4

There had to be clues in the courtyard. I figured that was a good place to start. There was the golf club Kip was clutching, and there were the indentions in the grass, circles about 2-inches in diameter in the lawn around the body.

What could have caused them? They were very consistent. I would have to take a picture of these clues. I made sure no one was around and took my cellphone out of my dress pocket. I snapped a pic and quickly put my phone back. I looked around some more, careful not to get my heels dirty. Why did I need comfortable shoes when I spent most of my shift sitting behind the concierge desk? I crept around some more but didn't find anything suspicious. Could the golf club be the murder weapon?

Who had a motive to kill Kip? Kip seemed to be loved by everyone. I tried to recall any arguments he'd had recently, and remembered one between him and Rich Gibbons, a programmer and start-up company enthusiast, last week in the foyer. If I thought about it long enough, I could probably remember what they were arguing about. I'd always tried to give residents their privacy, but when they're talking near the concierge desk it's impossible not to overhear.

I remembered noticing earlier that on Kip's right wrist there was a Fitbit that might contain valuable information. I began to lift the cover draped over him when a man cleared his throat behind me.

"Cassie," Eric said. I jumped. "You're not allowed around the corpse. And the front desk is flooded with residents demanding more information."

"Oh, no," I said, dreading the residents' wrath.

"Look, there's no more information at this time," said Eric. "So you can tell them that. Once we know more, we'll give you and the rest of the Parkstone crowd an update."

Crowd? You mean revered group? Something told me the detectives may not be too happy with the residents already. And the residents definitely weren't too happy with the detectives' 24-hour lockdown decision.

While I had Eric's attention, I thought this would be a good time to inquire about case details. "I noticed Kip was wearing a Fitbit," I said. "And I think the number of steps he took this morning could be an important clue to putting the puzzle pieces together."

"If that information becomes available, I'll let you know," he said. I didn't budge. He looked directly at me. "How's that?"

I felt like withering in his arms long enough to regain my resolve. "This is the worst thing that could happen at the Parkstone," I said.

"I know," he said, looking in my eyes. The sun was beginning to peek out of the clouds. "Do your best to take charge of the front desk. And we'll do our jobs. I promise you we'll find the murderer."

I thought that Eric was capable, and dreamy, but wasn't sure he understood the gravity of the situation. "You deal with murders every day. You're used to it. Something like this has never before happened at the Parkstone."

Eric put his arms on my shoulders. "It's a shock, but stay strong."

I took a deep breath and said to myself: *And don't give up solving the crime.*

CHAPTER 5

Back in the lobby, it was a zoo in a marble palace. Mr. Gillrot was banging on the large, gold lobby doors demanding to leave. Rich Gibbons who had recently had a verbal disagreement with Kip was standing visibly upset at the coffee station surrounded by a swarm of other residents.

"Cassie, we're out of dark roast," Rich said, the impatient line growing behind him.

"No, we're not," I said, hoping I hadn't spoken too soon. I opened the coffee station drawers and replenished the supplies. "Fortunately, we have more dark roast."

Rich grinned. *Phew*! Sometimes this job wasn't so bad. One happy resident.

I would be available for questions, too, but first things first: I needed to send notice to Baxter headquarters. I sat down at the computer to type a memo about the murder, although it could be a while until anyone at the New York headquarters read it.

Dear Mr. Baxter,

I regret to inform you that there has been a murder at the Parkstone. Highly esteemed resident Kip Ace was found dead in the courtyard around 9 a.m. this morning by yours truly.

It is with a sad heart that myself and the other residents are going about our day. We are also all going about our day together—whether we like it or not—because the lead detective on the case has put us on 24-hour lockdown. I made sure that the procedure complied with that listed in the policy manual. In addition to the murder, we have received numerous resident complaints about the water being shut off this morning, due to a leak in apartment 401. I have been told by maintenance that the water will be back on by noon.

Please let me know of any other items I should attend to. Thank you for your attention to these matters. I expect I will hear from you shortly.

Cassie Hall

They wouldn't be happy about this, not one bit. And neither was I. This murder had happened on my watch. Then I figured I shouldn't be complaining. It had to be worse for Kip's wife, Bunny Ace. Did she know?

I thought about her phone call this morning asking about her outfit, and my heart sank.

And then suddenly it dawned on me, Bunny Ace! She hadn't been told yet. She probably had no idea about Kip. Poor woman!

Just then the elevator door opened. There was a long pause as the lobby crowd stared in its direction. Out walked Bunny. Her usual gait was quick, but today she walked slowly, almost as if to stabilize herself. She was dressed in a white lace top, jeans and flip-flops. She was visibly agitated at her blond hair that seemed to fly in wisps around her face. At this point, everyone had turned to stare.

She made it over to the desk and used one arm to steady herself on the concierge counter. "Cassie, I heard the announcement. What's going on?"

And before I could get a word out, Bunny said, "I fear…"

And I, who was nervously fidgeting with my concierge tag because I couldn't look her in the eye, nodded. "Mrs. Ace, we're really sorry to have to tell you the news." Bunny fell forward on the counter, and I caught her just before her head hit the tough mahogany. She was in shock.

Eric walked over, taking Bunny's hand and putting his other arm around her shoulder. "Mrs. Ace, we have some bad news, but we're going to find who did this."

"That's all there is anymore," Bunny said. "Bad news." Eric could be seen telling her in a low voice about Kip, and Bunny pounded her fists against Eric's chest. "How did this happen? Why would someone do this to my Kip?"

"I assure you, we're doing everything we can to catch the killer." He walked her over to the far end of the lobby where they had more privacy. They talked in low mumbles. I made a tea for Bunny at the coffee station and shooed onlookers away. Even Mr. Gillrot had the decency to stay away and mind his business during this time.

Bunny was given access to the paramedics and assured that whatever she needed, we'd be able to provide it for her: food, warm blankets, and coffee or tea.

"The one thing you can do for me is catch the killer!" she said to Eric. "I'm mourning Kip and right now the only other thing I care about is that the killer is brought to justice."

The detectives spent the next twenty minutes interviewing her with me doing my best to listen in.

"He didn't have any enemies. At least not that I knew of," she said. "Although I wasn't always privy to his personal and professional affairs."

Eric leaned in, "Any recent threats?"

"Not that I can remember," she said. "He had a business deal with Rich Gibbons that recently fell through. You know, Rich from the fourth floor." She paused. "But I can't imagine the deal turned that sour."

"All of these details are important," said Eric. "We'll be looking for clues and building a case over the next 24 hours. Anything you remember—a disagreement, a new friend, a new venture. Tell us about it."

"You have my word," she said holding a wad of Kleenexes to her nose. "Anything for Kip."

CHAPTER 6

The noise complaint logged into the computer came from Rich Gibbons, the computer programmer, at 8:15 in the morning. That was technically the daytime concierge's shift, which started at eight. This was my responsibility. I had been so preoccupied with the water shut off that I hadn't even seen it until now.

I had just found a quiet moment to read it. Noise Complaint: Loud arguing between a man and a woman in the courtyard. Voices carried all the way to the fourth floor.

Had Rich seen who was fighting couple was? If it was Kip, which most likely it was, who could he have been fighting with so early in the morning? According to the complaint, it was a woman, but who? I would need to follow up with Rich about the noise complaint regardless, but maybe I could get even more information from him about the murder, too.

Rich was sitting in one of the plush chairs near the Halloween decorations in the lobby when I approached him. I had just finished putting the final touches on the decorations—witches, goblins and pumpkins— yesterday and was happy with the way they'd turned out.

I tapped him on one of his large, broad shoulders. He jumped. "Ahhh. You scared me."

"I'm sorry, I didn't mean to scare you," I said. Noted: he is on edge. "Do you mind if I sit down?"

"That's fine," he said. "I startle easily."

I had the noise complaint paper, which I'd printed out, in my hand. "I've been meaning to ask you about the noise complaint you filed this morning, only a few hours ago."

"Oh, yeah, I already forgot about that," he said. "But now that you bring it up, yeah that was annoying."

"Did you see who was in the courtyard?"

"No," he said. "That's why I said a disagreement between a man and woman. I couldn't see who was there among the trees."

The plush chairs were perfectly comfortable during this difficult conversation. I couldn't believe I was sleuthing! Rich could hold the clue to the courtyard mystery in his memory. If I could just hear him over the swarm of people in the lobby who were talking louder and louder, then my efforts would be off to a perfect start.

"Did you happen to hear what they were arguing about?" I said trying to drown out the cacophony.

"No, not a word. Just garbled echoes emanating from the courtyard," he said. "Seemed like she was yelling more than he was."

So, the killer could be a female. Which female would have a reason for killing Kip? I'd just have to find the answer to that and then cinch this case like a belted Prada gown.

"You can dig all you want. And I hope it's helpful. I'm going to tell the detectives the same thing when they ask," he said. He looked around the room. "Looks like they have their hands full interviewing people at the moment."

"Anything else you can remember from this morning?"

"The fighting was so loud I heard it with my balcony door closed," he said. "Whatever they were fighting about was fierce."

His hands began to shake and I felt as though maybe I had inquired too much. I wanted to ask about the disagreement that he and Kip Ace had had a couple of weeks ago, but thought better of it. The detectives would most likely be questioning him and that would be stepping on their toes. And I didn't want to step on the detectives' toes. At least not Eric's. Speaking of which, I'd have to find him and inquire again about the number of Fitbit steps. That could also be a crucial clue to the case.

Just then, shrieks pierced the air and Ginnie Langford, Bunny's best friend, embraced a mourning Bunny.

Information about the argument could wait until later.

Sobs from the two women filled the air as red strobe light-like lights from the detective cars danced on the marble flooring and ornate walls. I felt temporarily stuck in a disco club in Washington D.C. and not at one of Bethesda, Maryland's finest.

Ginnie was the opposite of Bunny. She had bright red curly hair and dressed in bold colors. She wore a signature headband everywhere—all the time—even when taking out the trash. She was more outgoing and took up space when she talked.

The two women cried into each other's arms as the detectives looked on, appearing bewildered as to what to do next.

Eric cleared his throat. "Mrs. Langford, we'd like to ask you a few questions."

Ginnie whipped around. "Can't you see I'm consoling my best friend?"

It looked more like she needed consoling herself by looking at the tears streaming down her face.

"I see that," said Eric. "It's just that we'd like to ask you a few questions about Kip. The sooner you answer our questions..."

"You have questions?" Ginnie said. "What about my questions? Like who killed Kip?"

The red strobe lights reflecting off the walls made my head hurt. And Ginnie and Eric's discussion was about to escalate.

My sleuthing had gone so well with Rich that I decided to jump in. I walked over to where they were sitting. "Ginnie, the detectives are trying to solve this case as quickly as possible. The sooner you answer the questions, the more likely the 24-hour lockdown will be lifted."

"And we'll all be happy?" Ginnie said, wiping away tears. "None of this changes the fact that Kip is dead."

Bunny looked taken aback and turned to Ginnie. "Just answer their questions. There's only a couple of them."

With that, Ginnie sat down with Eric. Luckily, I happened to be sitting in the velvet plush seat right next to her.

"How long had you known Kip?" Eric said.

"About as long as I've known Bunny," she said.

Eric looked up from his notebook, "How long is that?"

"About thirty years. Since college," she said, twisting a Kleenex into a knot and moving her long curly, red hair to one side.

Was she nervous or were these typical characteristics of hers? She continued to cry uncontrollably, even after Bunny left. It seemed personal for her, more than just consoling a best friend.

"Did you know if he had any enemies?" I said to Ginnie almost as a reflex. I'd heard the detectives ask it, and now it seemed liked the appropriate time. I also wanted to know the answer so thought I should go for it. Eric shot me a glance and said, "geeze," under his breath.

"He was loved by so many," she said. "His fans adored him. Bunny loved him." She broke into sobs again. "Unconditionally."

Then Ginnie tried to regain her composure. She adjusted her headband. And looked about the room. She was probably looking for Bunny who had stood up to stare out the large window to the courtyard.

"Only a few more questions," Eric said, trying to keep Ginnie focused. "Do you know of anyone who disliked him? Anyone who had a motive?"

Ginnie thought for a moment. "There's no one I can think of right now," she said.

Eric flipped his notebook shut with extra emphasis. "If you think of something, let me know."

She looked up at him and in a softer voice said, "I will come find you."

After that interview ended, Eric asked me to meet him at the concierge desk. He looked more upset with me than I'd ever seen him in fifteen years. "I know you're trying to help, but don't," he said, watching Ginnie walk away towards Bunny near the window.

I didn't appreciate the tone, especially on my turf. "I'm trying to help solve the case," I said. "I work in this building, I was on duty this morning and there has been a murder. I at least get the chance to solve it."

He glanced over in Ginnie's direction again. "There's something she's not telling us. And I need to find that out. But with you jumping in asking questions, that's not helping. Solving a case is really complex, and it's a process best left up to the professionals," he said. "That's me and the other guys who are here. As you've noticed, there's a strong detective presence here. So, while I appreciate your help with the questioning, back off."

I felt as tilted as my concierge nametag. "I was trying to help." I paused fighting back tears. "I'm just as capable of solving this crime as you and the other detectives on the case."

Eric put his notebook away in his back pocket. "You might be, but what I know is that you don't have the background training or the field experience. Plus, solving crimes is too risky for you, Cassie. This reminds me of when Hunter died, and you felt the responsibility for solving the case. You almost went crazy trying to remember the make of the car and the license plate."

"This isn't about Hunter," I said, somewhat lying. "And I'm not adverse to risks." I thought about how I'd landed this job and moved out to Bethesda, to be with him, hoping he'd be my soon-to-be fiancé. That move alone was a huge gamble. And remained so.

I continued, "You can try and deter me all you want, but if I solve the crime within 24 hours, the residents will be happy, and my boss Royce Baxter will be pleased, which are my prime responsibilities after all."

A tight-lipped smile graced Eric's face. "Can't argue with that."

I figured now was my chance to ask the question. "Any chance you checked the Fitbit steps?"

He slapped his forehead. "You have permission to yell at me later."

"How about now?" I asked with a grin. I took his hand from his forehead. "The sooner you get me the information, the sooner I can solve this case."

Eric squeezed my hand back. "You're unstoppable."

CHAPTER 7

The 30-year-old stone building had all five-star ratings on <u>apartments.com</u>, mainly because luxury was synonymous with life here at the Parkstone.

Rumor had it that Kip Ace loved living at the Parkstone so much that he wanted to continue renting after their mansion renovations were complete. I wondered how that affected his dynamic with Bunny and if the Aces fought about whether to return home.

Lillian, the leasing agent, would know all about that. From the door frame, I could see she was in her office, sorting through a stack of papers on top of her desk. When I walked in, she grabbed at the cane resting at her side.

"What can I do you for?" she said.

"We have quite the situation out there," I said, crossing my arms. "Lots of unhappy residents, and we're all stuck like this for the next day at the most whether we like it or not."

"I heard the overhead," she said, looking around her office, which was very neat and organized.

"You don't seem flustered at all," I said amazed.

"I wish I could talk," she said, "but again, I'm busy. Maybe I don't have enough time to be flustered."

"Do you know of anyone who would have wanted to harm Kip?"

"I'm too busy for this conversation," she said.

"How can you be too busy?" I said. "We're on lockdown. There's nothing to do."

"Look," she said, walking toward me with her cane. "I didn't know Kip all that well. The only thing I knew about him as a resident is that his lease was up and he and his wife couldn't agree on whether they wanted to re-sign and under what terms. Major disagreements." She shook her head. "Kip wanted to stay. She wanted to leave."

"And you were pushing them to sign?" I said.

"Of course I *wanted* them to sign," she said. "That's my job. That's what Royce Baxter and Company are expecting of me. To get people to sign leases."

"And?" I said. "How did they leave it?"

She sat back down in the chair, placing her cane on the side of the table, and threw up her hands. "That's all I know. What about you? How is everything going with the lockdown?"

"As well as it can be," I said. "Any help is much appreciated. I wrote a memo to headquarters but haven't heard back yet. Residents are getting restless and we still have about 22 hours left to go."

"Well don't let me keep you," she said.

I was getting the impression she really wanted me to leave. "And one more thing," I said. "There's a noise disturbance logged into the computer from this morning."

"Oh really?" she said, looking interested in the conversation for the first time. She actually looked fearful.

"It was reported that a female and a male were yelling at each other in the courtyard."

"This morning?" she said. "Kip?" She paused as if she was thinking about something deeper than the papers on her desk. She grabbed for her cane to stand up, then thought better of it. There was something different about her. "Well, good luck finding the female. Sixty percent of the building is female," she said.

Noted. And I was standing right in front of one. It was a very important clue. Could Lillian be the first suspect?

CHAPTER 8

Bunny found me in the sea of people. She looked me straight in the eye, which made me think this was the moment that Bunny was going to get upset with me for not answering the phone when she first called this morning. Bunny looked as if this was the most important thing she was ever going to say.

Still wiping tears away from her face, she said, "I've been meaning to tell you, we—Kip and I—were expecting a photographer to photograph his wine collection today. At 1 p.m."

"How can I help?" I asked, relieved it wasn't about the phone call.

"And, well, the photographer didn't answer his phone when I called him minutes ago to tell him the photo shoot was going to be cancelled." Ignored phone calls seemed to be a theme with Bunny. She continued. "I hate having to think of all this stuff, but I have to, you know?"

"Yes, of course," I said.

"Kip was so proud of his wine collection. It was his prize," she said. "He couldn't wait for this day to have all the white and red wines photographed. The collection was going to be featured in *Wine World*, you know?"

"I did know about the photo shoot," I said. "He had mentioned it once or twice in passing. I also know that Kip, uh Mr. Ace, had an extensive collection of wine. He mentioned it here and there. And I know his wine collection takes up about 40 percent of the entire resident wine cellars."

"Oh, dear, he loved it so," she said. "Why, he collected wines from all around the world. He bought wines from everywhere. Everywhere." Then she seemed to drift off into another world.

"Bunny, are you okay?" I said.

"Yes, I'm fine, dear. You're so sweet," she said. "This is all just so sudden." Then she seemed to regain her composure. "And if you could please let the photographer know, if he shows up at the lobby doors, what happened."

"I will," I said, still feeling like there was something she wasn't telling me. This is where detective training would come in handy like Eric mentioned earlier. "I promise. Anything else?"

She began to walk away and looked over her shoulder and said, "I know you will, dear," she said. "We are all bound by our word."

No less than an hour later, the photographer showed up. The knocking on the door to the lobby of the Parkstone was so loud it could be heard over the Bach concerto that was playing. Protocol stated that classical music was to be played in the lobby at all times. And this one was no different.

I ran to the lobby door to see who was knocking. Gilbert, the doorman, was taking a break on the other side of the lobby. There was a gentleman standing there with jeans, a polo shirt and sandals, with a camera slung around his neck and he was holding a tripod.

The photographer!

"Excuse me," I said to Eric, interrupting a conversation. "I need to go outside to speak with the photographer banging on the lobby doors. Strict instructions from Bunny."

"Be quick, all right?" he said. "Nobody's supposed to be allowed outside."

"You got it," I said.

Eric opened one side of the heavy doors and shut them immediately. I heard them lock again from the inside. I breathed in deep. It was good to be away from the fray even if it was for just a moment.

I gave the photographer a huge concierge smile like he had just said, "Say cheese!" "You must be the photographer for the photo shoot of Kip Ace's wine collection." I extended my hand.

He nodded. "And who are you? And why are the doors locked? I'm supposed to be here at one o'clock you know," he said shaking my hand.

"I'm the Parkstone concierge," I said. "I have some unfortunate news for you. This morning we were all saddened by the news that Kip Ace has been murdered."

He shook his head in disbelief. "Murdered?"

"Yes," I said, lowering my voice. "I know this comes as a shock. But he was murdered, this morning." I paused. "Needless to say, there won't be a photo shoot."

"My gosh, well, of course not. Wow, that's sobering," he said shaking his head in disbelief. "And Mrs. Ace, how is she holding up?"

"As best as can be expected," I said.

"He had quite the wine collection. Even had a real gem of a collector's item, a 1947 Chateau Cheval Blanc, which is so exclusive," he said. "Said he bought it from another resident." He shook his head in amazement. "Would have liked to have seen the dollar signs on that one."

"He bought it from a resident at the Parkstone?" I said thinking a resident wine exchange program wasn't such a bad idea.

"Yeah," he said, "Can't remember the seller's name."

"I don't know who that could have possibly been. I don't know any resident who was as much of a wine enthusiast as Mr. Ace."

"I'm truly sorry to hear about Kip's death," he said. "If I'm not needed for the photo shoot, I better be going on my way. Please give my best to Mrs. Ace."

"Of course," I said. "And please keep the murder to yourself for now. The news outlets will get a hold of it eventually, but for now Mrs. Ace has asked that the news be kept private."

"I'll put a cork in it," he said.

CHAPTER 9

After I told Mrs. Ace everything had been resolved with the photographer, I resumed my position at the front desk. I even had a moment to adjust my Cassie Hall name placard which had gotten slightly askew during all the commotion earlier. Moments later, the phone rang. I jumped at the noise. I was more rattled than I thought.

It was my mega boss, Royce Baxter.

"Cassie, I received your fax," he said. "While I'm stunned, keep in mind resident safety is of the utmost importance. And you are correct, the lockdown should not last more than 24 hours."

"We're holding up okay here, but the residents are getting restless," I said, trying to talk quietly. "And they're not too happy about the lockdown to say the least."

"It's for their own safety and to help with the investigation, so be sure to remind them of that. Do the detectives have any leads?"

"Not that I know of," I said, thinking I should probably check in with Eric soon.

"My dear, did the event—uh murder—happen last night or this morning?"

This is where I knew they could find fault with me. If Mr. Ace died when I was supposed to be in the courtyard making rounds, or when I didn't have an alibi, then my innocence outlook didn't look good.

"They believe it was in the morning, but they haven't pinpointed an exact time."

"And you were on duty, correct?"

"Yes," I said, upset with myself that I hadn't made myself more present during my shift. "But it also could have been during the wee hours of the morning, which would have been the night concierge shift."

"Did you hear anything strange or see anything out of place?"

"No," I said, remembering the scream and seeing a dark shadow flicker among the trees that caused me to run out to the courtyard in the first place. "Not a thing except Kip's dead body. And we did get a resident noise complaint from this morning from Rich Gibbons."

"It's important that you stay safe, have your wits about you and remind residents this will all be resolved shortly."

"I will," I said, knowing that the residents didn't want to listen. "Is there anything else I should know about operating the building during lockdown?"

"Close many of the amenities," he said. "For instance, the pool, the wine cellar, the courtyard, etc… Those should all be closed."

"Yes, of course sir," I said, hoping this situation would be resolved quicker than the Jacuzzi heated up in the winter. He seemed calm given the circumstances. Maybe that's because he was all the way at the company headquarters in New York City and not on the concierge front lines.

"The best thing you can do for the residents is stay calm," he said. "Offer to make them coffee or tea. One thing we're not doing is offering discounts on rent."

Royce Baxter, business-minded in any situation. I laughed. He must have read Mr. Gillrot's mind. "Yes, sir," I said.

At least the news was contained to the Parkstone residents, their families and the New York City headquarters. Just then, a newscaster on the TV on the wall behind me announced a story about a murder at the Parkstone. Residents robotically turned to stare. The footage had been taken from across the street. Oh great. Media, to add to the frenzy.

I was so distracted I almost forgot Royce was still on the phone. "Also, be sure to leave the sleuthing up to the detectives," he said. "The last thing we need is for you to be involved in the mystery even more than you already have been."

I said goodbye to Royce and tuned into the news coverage: "Parkstone residents are holed up in the building until the murderer is caught or the 24 hours is up. Talk about a bad set of circumstances for Parkstone residents, and a day of misery for golf lovers who just lost a great idol. Right now, we see three detective cars in front of the building. There were as many as eight earlier today. We got a look in through the lobby's front doors. Looks like residents are crammed in there like sardines, worse than the metro morning commute. They're talking to detectives who can hopefully solve this case."

I turned the TV off for the well-being of the residents and employees like myself. It was bad enough we were living the experience; we didn't need to re-live it on the news.

Next I took the noise violation and tapped Eric on the back. He didn't look like he wanted to leave the conversation, but then I motioned I had something to show him.

"It's so good to see you," he said as we walked over to the desk.

I pulled him in close so I could whisper, "Any more leads in the case?"

"Not a one," he said. "I'll tell you when we come across something."

I was sure he would. Eric was always trustworthy and reliable. He was the detective on watch at the Parkstone during the weekend day shifts, and he and I had experience teaming up to solve the building's mysteries.

Together we had solved the mystery of a strange noise coming from the first floor, the mystery of a leak in the lobby ceiling, and the mystery of a missing muffin from the leasing agent's desk. Turned out Jet-Setter was the culprit in the latter who-done-it. All of these mysteries we solved together. This one would be no different.

"Did you get the Fitbit information?" I said as Jet-Setter scrambled to her feet and trotted on the table between me and Eric.

"I forgot," he said. "Okay? I've been a little busy." The lobby was still packed.

"If you get the Fitbit information," I said, "I have my hands on the courtyard noise complaint that came in this morning."

"What?!" he said. "You have information you haven't told me about?"

"You didn't ask," I said. "And now I have bargaining power."

"You know it's obstruction of justice to withhold information from detectives, right?" he said.

"I'm not withholding it," I said, "It's right here." I waved the paper around.

"You always know how to make your point," he said.

"And all I want in return is to know how many steps were logged on Kip's Fitbit at the time of death."

"If you must know the number of steps was 613," he said.

I gasped. "So you did know, you just didn't want to tell me!"

"I don't want to see you get so involved in this case––head over your Jimmy Shoo shoes," he said.

"Choo," I said. "It's Jimmy Choo."

"Well, you know what I mean," he said. "This is detective work. And you're not a detective. You're an excellent concierge." I was not appreciating his condescending speech, but he continued. "And when was the last time you heard about a concierge solving a crime?"

"Never," I said as Jet-Setter scurried past my feet and darted toward his food bowl.

"Because concierges don't solve crimes," he said.

"Except for this one." I started to walk away, happy I'd gotten the Fitbit information.

"Where are you going?"

"I have a crime to solve," I said, kicking up one of my heels.

CHAPTER 10

Now I had two clues to investigate. There was the Fitbit steps number and the noise complaint. Two pieces that could help solve this mystery. I decided to start with the Fitbit information first.

There were 613 steps. Since I had a Fitbit of my own, I knew that each night Fitbit resets automatically. So that 613 was the number of steps Kip had walked that morning. That was a lot more steps than from Kip's 12th floor apartment to the courtyard. I hadn't actually walked the steps yet, but I suspected that was true, which meant the courtyard hadn't been Kip's first destination. He must have stopped somewhere else first!

I decided to allow about 40 steps for walking around in his apartment before leaving. That left 573 steps to go from his apartment to another destination and then to the courtyard. I figured I could leave the concierge desk unmanned for a couple of minutes while I logged steps into my Fitbit to deduce where Kip could have gone.

Re-tracing his steps could prove essential to solving his murder.

I took the elevator to the 12th floor and walked down to the 10th floor, to where Mr. Gillrot lived, for example, but it wasn't enough steps. Between those two places and the courtyard, it didn't add up to 613 steps.

I tried walking from the 12th floor to the fourth, where a lot of tenants questioned by the detectives lived. I was midway down the fourth floor hallway when I heard the patter of footsteps. I wasn't alone.

I reached for my cellphone in case I needed to call Eric. My hands trembled. As I sped up, the footsteps behind me began to quicken. Then after taking one more step there was a loud noise and the hallway went dark. The footsteps stopped.

I fumbled to turn on my phone's flashlight app which created a small circle of light on my feet as I found my way to the stairwell. At least I was only on the fourth floor. There wasn't too much farther to go!

I had to re-gain my composure after the lights had gone out. It wasn't easy. My hands were shaking so much I was afraid my manicure would shake off. I listened again for the footsteps, but it was silent. I reminded myself the noises could be from a resident walking down the hall back to their apartment. But the murder had me on high alert. Whoever was behind me must have lost interest in following me or gotten scared off by the black-out. Near the stairwell, I almost mis-stepped, falling onto the ground or against the wall-papered hallway. I still had four flights left and it wasn't easy in my Jimmy Choo's. Once in the stairwell, I stepped down the flights of stairs as quickly and gingerly as I could, hoping I wouldn't twist an ankle in my heels.

Once I got to the lobby and saw the detectives trying to contain the crowd, something dawned on me: Maybe what I had experienced wasn't a power outage due to weather? Maybe someone—like a disgruntled resident––had intentionally caused the outage.

The lobby was filled with the same cacophony as Grand Central Station. Detectives waved their arms in an attempt to get the residents to listen. I grabbed Eric's arm. "What's the next step?"

"Thank God, you're here," he said, placing his large hands on my shoulders. "I was worried about you."

"I was trying to re-trace Kip's steps," I said. "When the black-out happened. There were footsteps behind me."

"Where were you?"

"The fourth floor," I said, twisting a heel off, to check for blisters. "So, not far. But someone was treading cautiously behind me."

"You didn't see who it was?" he said looking incredulous.

"No! I didn't turn around to look," I said. "Before I knew it, the lights were out and I was fumbling my way down the stairs."

"I'm glad you're okay," he said. "I don't think it's safe for you to investigate this case alone."

"But I'm *not* investigating this case alone," I said. "You and the rest of the detectives are investigating it with me."

"I'm worried about you," he said putting his warm hand against my cheek.

"But we have to find out who did this," I said.

"We will. But I need *you* to cooperate, and that means stop investigating on your own. It's dangerous."

From what I could see with the light filtering in through the lobby's high windows, Eric was looking directly into my eyes. I believed he was worried about me, but I needed to continue my investigation.

He continued, "Look, we got some leads," he said. "I'll tell you later, all right? Right now, I need you to find the breaker panel. This blackout is about to cause an uprising."

I was proud that I actually knew where the breaker panel was. It had been part of my online training with Baxter Enterprises. And it had served me well! Good thing when I took the class, I wasn't just thinking of the Tiffany's earrings I wanted, or the next blouse I was going to hand pick for Mrs. Canterbury. Or that ever important ring from Eric.

The back communal room was a mess! *It would be a good idea to let Lillian work her "clutter to clean" magic here,* I thought as I used the flashlight app to guide me around boxes and mounds of papers stacked up on the floor. I finally made it to the back wall where the breaker switches were when I heard scuffling. Then footsteps. Again!

I shined the flashlight on the room's doorway. "Anybody there?" I said nervously, digging one of my heels into the oriental carpet. There was no response. I fumbled for the breaker panel, my hand shaking nervously. Found it! I was about to turn on the lights when I heard a large crash. It came from the other room.

It startled me. Luckily, I didn't drop my phone and used the light app to guide me to the office next to Lillian's, where Lillian lay on the floor under a large box.

"My fault," she said. "I thought I could reach it."

"Are you all right?"

"This office is a mess. I don't understand why someone would have placed the large boxes on top," she said.

"I agree," I said. "Any chance you want to use your organizational skills around this office?"

She gave me a weary look.

"I'll pick out a Kate Spade dress just for you," I said. "I even have one in mind. It's a symmetrical shape with buttons and a fox pattern print."

"I think I can manage something," she said.

I was learning quickly that my side business of being a personal shopper to residents and employees was coming in handy. I smiled and then left politely. I had lights to bring on!

I made it back to the breaker panel in the other room. I had learned about resetting the breakers during on-boarding, and even reset them one time before when the power had gone out due to inclement weather. This time was different. It was crisp and cool outside now, but it wasn't raining or windy. Something told me this power outage was due to something more sinister, such as a short circuit culprit who'd tampered with the insulating wires.

When I made it back to the front of the breaker panel, I followed the steps I remembered from the training video.

I took a deep breath. *Here it goes.* I then turned each breaker back on.

And then—to my relief—the lights came back on. I exhaled deeply. The Parkstone wasn't in the dark anymore, except for the identity of the lurking murderer.

As far as I was concerned, I'd thwarted their plan. *Take that disgruntled resident, or murderer.*

I made my way back to the lobby to see the residents' smiling faces.

"You did it!" said Eric. "You're the best."

"I'd say you're the best if you tell me more information you've discovered about the case."

"Shhh," he said. "We have to keep it quiet. All of this is confidential, all right? The boys would never let me forget it if I jeopardized top secret information."

"I'll keep your information as secret as a fall collection show in the summer."

He looked bewildered.

"If you knew anything about fashion, you'd know that's pretty secret," I said.

"Well, all right," he said, still not looking convinced. Eric looked at me with his eyes as dark as the waters of Colorado's Black Lake. "We have more information," he said. I got nostalgic for a moment. And I thought back to the good old days, before Hunter's death, when everything in life was perfect. The hiking and camping trips, all the fun places to hang out downtown.

Those were good days. "Do tell," I said, noticing how his brown cuffed shirt matched his pants, which matched his socks. Eric was a snazzy dresser. Always put together, even in his detective outfit during times of duress. He was also consistent. He'd stuck by me all those years I'd been a mess after Hunter's death. I closed the door to make sure Lillian didn't hear us discussing the case. This was sensitive information. "It was a blunt object," he said.

"A golf club!" I said, not able to contain myself, and probably guessing what every other detective already knew. "And he was found with a golf club, so that makes sense."

"Not necessarily," he said. "You'd be surprised. I've seen cases where the obvious answer is not the right one."

"And the least obvious answer would be?" I said, mulling it over.

"Could be a lot of things," he said. "That's where the detective work comes into play."

"I'll do my best to think up all the possible answers and then narrow them down."

He squirmed. "Some of the best detectives on the case don't know what the object is yet."

"My gut says golf club," I said because that did seem to be the most obvious answer. But I was sure going to be on the lookout for other objects that fit the bill.

"Will you be able to get more information on this matter?"

"Possibly," he said, "But it's not guaranteed we'll have more information right away."

"I was in the middle of investigating the Fitbit steps when the power went out," I said. "I heard footsteps behind me."

"Could have been someone walking back to their apartment," he said.

"I got this creepy feeling I was being followed," I said.

"Most likely a tenant," he said.

"The most obvious answer isn't always the right one," I said. "Didn't you just tell me that?"

He put his arm around my shoulder. "Look, I'm trying not to scare you," he said. "We're doing the best we can to keep everything under control. It might be best if you man the concierge desk for a while. Give the sleuthing a break."

"That's fine," I said. "I can sleuth from the concierge desk. I also owe some residents items from my wardrobe. I owe Lillian the red fox Kate Spade dress," I said. "And it would be nice of me to bring something for Bunny. She must be going through such a difficult time. Maybe a scarf would be a nice gesture."

"Are you still running your fashion consultant business on the side?" he said.

"I'm more of a personal shopper. Clothes have a magical effect on people," I said, thinking about how I hoped to one day work in fashion design.

"So does someone I know," he said, smiling at me.

"Oh stop it," I said blushing. I opened the door because I was feeling hot. A small line had formed at the concierge desk and I knew that was my cue to jump back in. I'd run upstairs to get the clothes later sometime when I needed to take a quick break. For now, I was Cassie the cheery concierge.

"And Eric?"

"Yes," he said.

"If you hear anything?"

"You'll know what I know," he said.

Somehow, for the first time, that wasn't comforting.

CHAPTER 11

A small line of residents had formed at the concierge desk and it made my hands sweat. I snatched the, "Will Be Back Shortly," sign away from the counter. I was back, and ready to handle resident complaints. And just because that task had to be an uphill battle, the first resident in line was Mr. Gillrot. "When is the 24-hour ban going to be lifted?" he said, looking more gaunt and haggard than the previous two hours.

"When the day is up," I said, hoping the conversation didn't go on forever.

He was shaking his hands in the air. "That's not good enough."

"When would you like it to be over?" I said.

"Now!" he retorted. "Right now."

"That's not possible," I said, "Unfortunately, the detectives first need to catch whoever did this. Can you remember any clues from last night or this morning that might be pertinent to the case? That might help it go quicker."

"No, sireee," he said. "I remember I had plans to visit my family today."

Family was important to Mr. Gillrot. He visited them every weekend. They were all he had. They were his better half.

"I'm sorry," I said. "I really am."

"Doesn't cut it," he said. "I had plans to visit my family today and instead I'm packed in here like a cigarette in the Parkstone lobby."

"You also have the option of going to your apartment," I said, wishing I also had a keen eye for men's clothing. I'd handpick a fancy tuxedo for him and hopefully end the torment.

"If I wanted to spend the time in my apartment, I would, don't you think?"

There was no consoling Mr. Gillrot.

"I bet you we're going to be out of here in less than 24 hours," I said. "We're going to find the killer before then."

"We?" he said. "Meaning you and the detectives?"

"That's right," I said. "I've been helping with the case. And we're not going to stop investigating until justice is served."

"I regret the day I even rented here!" Mr. Gillrot said. "And I hope you don't get in over your fashionista head."

"Next complaint," I said, knowing that if I didn't take control of the concierge desk, Mr. Gillrot wouldn't stop complaining, and I'd be stuck listening to him for the rest of the afternoon.

The next resident in line was Kelly Cartwright. She was the Parkstone's only wheelchair resident. She was fierce and would zip around in her wheelchair as quick as a jaguar. She wheeled up to the concierge desk.

"This news is flying faster than an object breaking the sound barrier," Mrs. Cartwright said.

"So I take it you've heard," I said, leaning over the desk to meet her eye to eye.

"I've heard. Have I ever!" she said smiling.

How could she be smiling?

"Heard it first thing this morning and haven't been able to stop smiling ever since," she said.

"A man died," I said.

"A wretched self-absorbed man," she said, "who would never let me forget that I once ran over his big toe."

"What?" I said. "You mean there was an altercation between you and Mr. Ace?"

"If you call me accidentally—accidentally—running over his big toe an altercation, then, yes, that's what we had," she said, using her arms wildly as she spoke.

"Well, I'm sorry to hear that," I said. "Everything I've heard about Mr. Ace is that he was really nice."

"I'm sorry to tell you, Cassie," she said,. "but you heard wrong. He blamed me for his foot injury which prevented him from playing in the Congressional Easter tournament."

"Oh, geez," I said. "That's horrible. For both of you."

"I said I was sorry," she said. "The lobby floor was slippery that day and I was going fast and I skidded right over his big toe. Not on purpose, of course."

The more and more I saw Mrs. Cartwright's anger, the more I began to realize that she had a motive. She definitely had a long-standing feud with Mr. Ace. And the Congressional Easter tournament was a big one for Kip to miss. There was obviously bad blood between them. There was no tiptoeing around it. Pun intended.

"From then on, I couldn't stand to look at him. He even once called me Mrs. Cart*wrong*," she said. "Get it? Instead of Cart*wright*."

"I get it," I said, having no idea that Kip had it in him to say such a thing.

"Now you can see why I don't think much of him," she said. Then she gave it some thought. "And he didn't think much of me."

Kelly Cartwright definitely had a motive. But did she have the force necessary to wield a golf club to kill Kip? I'd need to start investigating the murder weapon too. Was the murder weapon even a golf club? And if it wasn't a golf club that killed Kip Ace, what could it have been?

Mrs. Cartwright said goodbye and wheeled away with such fierceness that I thought she might run over another toe!

Then, third in line was Mrs. Canterbury. And she was wearing the rose floral blouse that I'd picked out for her a week ago. She looked fabulous!

"Mrs. Canterbury," I said. "Compliments on your blouse; it looks stunning."

"Why, thank you, dear," she said. "Someone with great taste picked it out for me. I'm just wondering if there's any way I can get out and go to the grocery store. It's right across the street."

I took a step back. I hadn't thought about the residents not having enough food to eat in their apartments.

Mrs. Canterbury looked up and grinned sheepishly. "Our maybe we can order in?"

"Good point," I said. There were a ton of take-out menus in the desk drawer. "I'll ask the detectives. Maybe we can order from Ploy's Pizzeria right next door."

"That would be lovely," she said.

"And are you feeling better from fainting earlier?"

"Yes," she said. "Still a bit winded. But hanging in there."

CHAPTER 11

I couldn't let the Parkstone residents go hungry, so I ordered six large pizzas—a combination of pepperoni, vegetable and plain—to be delivered to the Parkstone building early that afternoon. The antsy residents couldn't wait. I was hoping the pizza smell and deliciousness of the pizzas would help take their minds off the case. I, on the other hand, couldn't stop thinking about it.

There were more people than I thought who were upset with Mr. Ace: Mrs. Cartwright for starters. And then there was Mr. Gillrot, who was upset with everyone—life included. And then there was Lillian, who I suspected was up to no good.

Everyone seemed to be enjoying the pizza from Ploy's Pizzeria, which had been voted the best pie in the Washington, D.C., metro area. After the Pizzeria heard about what had happened at the Parkstone, they even added extra toppings free of charge. Mr. Gillrot already had had two slices of pepperoni, and Mrs. Cartwright had snagged a slice of vegetable. Then Mr. Gillrot appeared in line again right behind Mrs. Canterbury. Was he back for seconds already? Or was he up to no good?

He motioned with his hands that there was space for Mrs. Canterbury to move up in line. "Move up," he said.

"I will, when they're done," she said, crossing her arms, annoyed with Mr. Gillrot's pushiness.

"Well, you've got to get a slice," he said. "That's all I'm saying."

"I'm going to," she said, turning around to see if anyone else was overhearing his strange behavior. I wondered if I should jump in and say something. But sometimes it was best to let the residents solve things on their own.

"The pizza might be all gone by the time you get up there," he said. "And why wouldn't you get a slice? They're free."

"If you would just hold your horses," Mrs. Canterbury said.

From where I stood behind the concierge desk, the line wasn't moving all that quickly. Free didn't mean fast.

Mr. Gillrot looked agitated. "Well it's the least they could do for us, having us locked up here under these circumstances," he said. "That's why I didn't just take one slice. I took two."

Mrs. Canterbury looked as though she was trying to tune him out.

"It's not like you have to buy anything," Mr. Gillrot said. Mr. Gibbons in front of them was oblivious to their bickering and took his time selecting a slice. After all, there was no rush.

Mrs. Canterbury scowled at Mr. Gillrot. "You should have taken ten pizza slices," she said. "Then you'd be far away in your apartment, eating them all day and the rest of us wouldn't have to be bothered by you!"

Mr. Gillrot frowned—a slow, all-knowing frown—as if to say, "So that's the way it's going to be." I knew Mrs. Canterbury's frustration. Mr. Gillrot would spend hours sometimes stuck to the concierge desk like a barnacle, talking my ear off about the news, his family, and wine. And now it looked as though he knew he was getting on Mrs. Canterbury's last nerve in the same fashion.

Then he threw up his hands in the air and said, "Get ten slices! Why not?" he said. "They're free!"

Mrs. Canterbury shook her head as if she'd given up. "What is your obsession with free and with being such a curmudgeon?" Then, before Mr. Gillrot could respond, Mrs. Canterbury glared right at him as if daring him to respond.

That was a no-win situation for Mr. Gillrot. One point for Mrs. Canterbury. And at least all the pizza was getting eaten.

Their interactions amused me for a good portion of the early afternoon. And it was good to know there was someone who could stand up to Mr. Gillrot if need be. Manning the free pizza table was a lot more difficult than I'd ever imagined it could be, topped with all the residents' personalities. I wondered how easily Mr. Gillrot's anger could turn into rage, like I saw him turn on Mrs. Canterbury.

CHAPTER 12

Mrs. Canterbury took another slice of vegetable pizza. "Any leads?" she said.

"I'm not even supposed to be investigating the case," I said, taking a bite of pepperoni. "But of course I am."

Mrs. Canterbury smiled an all-knowing smile. "And?"

"I don't have any leads yet."

"And only twenty hours left," she said, putting the pizza slice onto her plate. "Start the wheels turning."

"That might not be enough time," I said, doubting that I'd be able to come up with the right person by then.

"It has to be," she said, shaking the pizza slice in my direction. Mrs. Canterbury was a slow eater.

"If only we had more clues," I said, wiping my hands on a napkin. "Surely someone must have seen something."

Mrs. Canterbury put the pizza slice down. "Well, there is something."

Plotting over pizza. I loved it! "Do tell," I said.

"It was a long time ago now though," she said. "A couple of months ago." She thought about it some more. "Actually, it was last summer. It was a year ago to be exact."

That's about the time the Aces moved into the Parkstone. "What happened?" I said, knowing that she had a gem of a clue.

"The tabloids! That's what happened."

"How do I not remember any of this?" I said.

"Oh yes," she said. "It was all over the tabloids."

"Mr. Ace?" I said.

"On the front covers. Mr. Ace, oh yes, Mr. Ace," she said gently shaking her head.

I had lost my appetite. I didn't want to hear any more bad news about my golf idol.

"What did they say?" I said even though a part of me didn't want to know. Kip Ace had been an idol of mine since I was young. And I still idolized him. I didn't want anything to get in the way of that.

Mrs. Canterbury put the pizza plate near the vase on the side table next to us. There was something much more important she had to focus her attention on.

"There was a photo of him sitting across from Bunny on their balcony looking very upset. Very angry. Brows furrowed. He looked as if he'd just lost a major tournament," she said.

"And they were on their balcony here?" I said. "The photo was taken from their apartment at the Parkstone?"

"Yes," she said. "And it wasn't paparazzi."

"How do you know?"

"The photo was at eye level," she said.

It was beginning to make sense. "So, it was taken by someone on a balcony at the same level as their apartment?"

"Exactly!" she said, pointing a knobby finger at me.

"I don't believe it," I said.

"You must," she said. "If you don't, Google Kip Ace and *National Inquirer* and the article and photo are right there."

My head felt light. This was all too much for me to handle.

A photo of Kip mad at Bunny? And a fellow resident snapping the angry picture? For what? To sell it to the tabloids and make money off a fellow resident?

I had to investigate. I contemplated reaching out to Eric and decided against it. He and the other detectives probably had their own leads to follow. Now—thanks to Mrs. Canterbury—I had mine.

I went to the business room on the first floor and found it was empty. Perfect for investigating. I Googled what Mrs. Canterbury had said and sure enough, there was a photo of Mr. Ace snarling at Bunny on their balcony with the caption: "Killer Golf Snub." The photo was taken at the same level and from the side. So, judging from the angle, it must have been someone who had an apartment on the 12th floor and on the right side of the building facing the crabapple courtyard.

I snuck back to the concierge desk and pulled out Parkstone's large binder full of floor plans and building assignments. The right courtyard side of the 12th floor were the even numbers 1210-1250. That meant there were five possible apartments with balconies on that side. I flipped to another page to find apartment assignments. Three of the five apartments were vacant, which left me with two apartments. One, closer to Mr. Ace's apartment, and one at the far end.

Either could have been the location of where someone had snapped the photo.

I ran back to the business room to look at the photo again on the screen. It couldn't have been from the closer apartment because the Ace's would have noticed the novice paparazzi. Also, the shot showed them almost both in silhouettes. A photograph from the closer apartment would have shown Bunny's side view and Mr. Ace's face full on.

After pinpointing the apartment as the far end one, I ran back to the concierge desk. With a thud I brought the binder back up onto the desk. The farther away apartment was Apt. 1250. I gasped. That was Mr. Gillrot's!

"Any luck?" Mrs. Canterbury said, grinning widely.

I shut the binder quickly, placing it back under the desk.

"Nope," I said. "I wish. I did see the photo though. Kip looks menacing. I've never even seen that expression on his face after a bad swing." It was better to keep this clue revelation from Mrs. Canterbury for the time being, just until I could talk with Eric and do more sleuthing.

"It's just awful, dear, that someone would take advantage of Mr. Ace like that."

"I agree," I said, knowing just who that someone was.

"You'll figure it all out," she said as she walked away with a smile. Now I was going to investigate. I tried to spot Mr. Gillrot in the crowd. But I couldn't find him. He must have gone back to his apartment— which earlier I had regretfully told him to do after the pizza fiasco. Maybe he was watching from his balcony, doing more spying of his own.

I hoped Bunny wasn't in danger of being in the tabloids any more than she already was. I was wondering if I should warn her about Mr. Gillrot and his potential to be very dangerous. I didn't want to see a picture of Bunny with the caption "Golfer's Widow Weeps" gracing the cover of the *National Inquirer*.

Also, why would Mr. Gillrot be taking advantage of Kip in the first place? Did he need money? But why sell out a fellow friend and resident? I knew Lillian had mentioned a couple of times that Mr. Gillrot had been really late paying rent. But to take advantage of Kip Ace? That was unheard of. I guess unheard of, until now.

The lobby had quieted down as the residents retreated to their apartments after the pizza. The detectives were still mulling around the lobby, interviewing the remaining residents. I got Eric's attention.

"Any leads?" I said.

"Not really," he said. "Not yet at least. Investigating can take some time." He paused. "Only thing is we don't have much of it."

I felt guilty, knowing that I had a possible lead that I had decided not to tell Eric about. At first I thought it would be great to share the information with him, but then what if it got into the wrong hands and the clue no longer became a lead? I wanted to investigate it first. Then if I needed his back up I'd let him know, but I couldn't let this lead get away from me.

He snapped his fingers. "Are you okay? You seem like you're dazing."

"I'm fine," I said. "Really, I'm fine. It's just that I still can't believe Mr. Ace has left us." I lowered my voice. "And that someone in the building could have done it."

"Someone in the building did do it," Eric said. "Coroner's Office placed time of death at 8:30 this morning."

I gasped. "Had I been on time for rounds this morning, I would have been there, or at least seen someone leaving the scene of the crime. There are only two doors that lead to the courtyard."

"I know it's difficult to grasp," he said. "But don't start thinking 'I should've this or I should've that.' That will only work against you. Seriously, that's the worst thing you can do. And right now, we need you and everyone else in this building to be at your best." He paused. "And it worries me to think that if you *had* been on time for rounds, you would have been there with the murderer and Kip. Anyone willing to kill someone is willing to kill another person to cover their tracks."

I liked that Eric was worried about me, but I didn't want him to worry at the same time. I shook my head. "I still wish I'd been there, or seen something that would help with the case."

"There's something else I've been meaning to tell you," he said. "Visitor time logs and resident interviews show there were no visitors from yesterday or early today who hadn't already left the building."

"That means..." I said.

"Yes, the crime was definitely committed by someone who lives in the building. It's been confirmed."

I shook my head again. "I just can't believe that someone in the Parkstone did it. Someone I've seen walking in and out of the lobby doors, and checking their mail, and commenting about the lobby's blaring classical music was someone who took Kip's life."

The gravity of it all was sinking in.

"I know, I told you this was tough work," Eric said, pulling my head into his chest as tears rolled down my cheeks.

"Many of the residents are shaken up, too," he said. "I know he was important to you."

"Do you know he signed an *Ace It*! book for me when I was seven? My mother and I had gone to the Cherry Creek Country Club to hear him speak. And when I saw him the first day he and Bunny moved in I was brave enough to ask him for his autograph. He didn't hesitate. Here's the brochure," I said, handing it to Eric. "It says, 'Stay out of life's bunkers.'"

It seemed as though Kip had found himself in one of his own.

"That's good advice," Eric said. "Maybe that bunker is the dangers of investigating the crime."

"I wouldn't take it that far," I said. Just then my eye caught Mr. Gillrot in line at the coffee station.

"I should get back to manning the concierge desk," I said. Eric looked surprised, almost hurt.

"Well, don't let me keep you," he said.

I had a mission to accomplish: launch an investigation into the whiner, Mr. Gillrot. He looked pleasantly happy at the coffee station, but I didn't let that fool me. There were many ways I could approach this situation, and I decided to go for the one that was the most direct. "Mr. Gillrot," I said, "were you the resident who took the photo of Kip and his wife and submitted it to the *National Inquirer*?" Then I braced for the response.

"No," he said, shaking his head. "By all means, no. I have no idea what you're talking about." The coffee machine had just stopped and Mr. Gillrot took his mug and added creamer.

"There's a photo of Kip glaring at Bunny and it was published in the *National Inquirer* last year," I said, very sternly, knowing my concierge title was not the end all be all of authority at the Parkstone.

"Well, that's difficult to do unknowingly, don't you think?" he said. "But it wasn't me."

I gave him a suspicious look. He continued. "Promise."

"So then how did the damaging photo of Kip get to the *National Inquirer*?"

"Someone sent it in," he said. "Don't you see? How else?"

"Who then?" I said, watching as he carefully cupped his coffee mug. "I have every reason to believe that photograph was taken by you."

"What makes you think that?" he said, taking a sip.

"The angle and the height. It must have been someone whose apartment was perfectly level with the Ace's."

Mr. Gillrot's head looked like it was about to explode. The coffee mug began to tremble.

"It *was* you!" I shouted. Some people in the lobby turned around to see what all the commotion was about.

"Ssssshhhh, will you?" he said. "Look, you're right. I took the picture, but I didn't send it to the *National Inquirer*. Are you happy?"

"Then how did someone else get their hands on it?"

"I didn't have a working computer at the time," he said. "I wanted to see how the photos turned out and the only option I had was to use the business room computer here on the first floor."

"Why even take the picture in the first place?" I said, feeling bad that I had wrongly accused Mr. Gillrot.

"He is—or was—a big celebrity. And they were arguing pretty loud. That's what got me out on the balcony in the first place," he said. "I thought about selling it for money. Or keep it for blackmail, for money."

There seemed to be a theme with Mr. Gillrot: money.

I couldn't decide whether I trusted Mr. Gillrot or not. What were the chances that he had the photo but wasn't the one who sent it to the *National Inquirer*? My guess was the chances were as slim as a high fashion runway model. Size zilch. I just had to figure out how to prove it.

He continued. "I left the photo on the computer's desktop and someone must have found it and decided to make money from it," he said. "I hope they got a pretty penny for it."

I gasped. "Mr. Gillrot, please don't say such things. Mr. Ace was a respectable man, and anyone who decided to profit from his marital struggles ought to be ashamed of themselves."

"When your wake-up call is three in the morning because they're arguing, tell me you wouldn't want to turn those fights into fortune."

"I don't know why we're arguing about this if it wasn't you!" I said. "Unless..."

He scowled. "I already told you what I know. And you're not even a detective." He shook one of his knobby fingers at me. "I ought to let the detective force know that you're digging your pampered nose where it don't belong."

I gasped again. If anything was down-to-earth at the Parkstone, it was me. Mr. Gillrot was more ornery than I ever thought. As far as I was concerned, I was doing just as good a job as the detectives, and Eric didn't mind me investigating anymore. He might have worried about me at first, but I guess he assumed he couldn't control my sleuthing. Mr. Gillrot was upset because I had found a clue to the puzzle that cast him in a disagreeable a light.

CHAPTER 13

I was sitting at the concierge desk when the digital photo slider on the counter caught my eye. Each photo displayed for about three seconds before flipping to another photo.

I remember thinking it was a great way for the building to showcase residents and events. The photo showing now was of a group of residents—Bunny and Ginnie included—outside on the pool top. Every member of the group was smiling. The good ol' days at Parkstone.

Then the photo dissolved out and there he was— Kip! Kip was in the next photo smiling in the courtyard, leaning against a golf club and holding a copy of his book *Ace It*! in his other hand. He looked relaxed. A golf ball rested at his feet.

That's the way he always looked. Perfectly content. How could such a happy, wealthy man get caught up in something that would end in his death?

Then the photo dissolved and another photo appeared. This one was of management—Lillian resting against her cane with her other arm resting on the concierge desk. This had been taken last October. She was dressed in a witch's hat and black dress for the Parkstone Halloween party called "Trick-o-Suite" held in the building's penthouse suite. Lillian had even borrowed a broomstick from the maintenance closet. She looked mean in the photo. I wouldn't want to be a resident going up against her during rent time.

The photo slider caused me to get lost in a reverie, and then I snapped out of it. Kip! I had to focus on the case. Taking out the photo of him in the courtyard would be a good idea. Bunny's mourning shouldn't be thwarted by an errant photo placement. I'd remove it right away, so as not to cause her any pain.

As I grabbed the digital photo album, I saw Mrs. Canterbury from across the way coming toward me.

She approached the desk. "I don't mean to be nosy," she said, "but what's happening with the fundraiser tomorrow? My niece was scheduled to compete, but with everything that's happened, I doubt the tournament will still be held."

"The tournament!" I said. I had completely forgotten. There was a charity tournament to fight cancer, and Kip was the golf celebrity spearheading it. So much work had already gone into the tournament that it was a pity not to have it. Even I had helped by designing the t-shirts, putting my fashion skills to good use. But how could there be a tournament without its host—Kip?

Mrs. Canterbury shook her head. "And I know you made those lovely t-shirts for it. I would love for my niece to still have one if that's all right."

Oh gosh. I looked through my emails quickly and saw that the Committee had emailed me to tell me the tournament had been cancelled. There was also a disclaimer that we'd have to mail the shirts to all the pre-paid participants. If Mrs. Canterbury wanted her niece's t-shirt today that would be one less shirt to mail.

Kip had chosen me as the designer and I had designed a trendy silkscreen printed t-shirt with the words "Fore A Cure." The 'o' in 'fore' was a golf ball. Kip loved it. I had already given him his shirt, which he'd been wearing when I'd found him. I remembered him saying that the shirts had turned out even better than he'd expected.

"You know what, Mrs. Canterbury?" I said. "I know they've cancelled the tournament. But I can get your niece a t-shirt. I have hundreds of pre-shrunk 100% cotton "Fore A Cure" shirts in my walk-in closet." This was one of those times I really appreciated working in the same building where I lived: convenience.

Mrs. Canterbury smiled. "You are such a dear."

"It's the least I can do. At least until this madness is over," I said.

Then she looked around with eyes suspiciously narrowed and lowered her voice. "Any leads that you know of?" she said with a daring smile.

"Not one," I said. "I'm hoping they wrap it up soon, but in all honesty, we may all be here until nine a.m. tomorrow."

"Good grief," she said. "I didn't think the detectives were serious about that 24-hour lockdown."

"If there's anything I can do to make it a more pleasant experience for everyone, let me know."

"My dear, you should be running the show," she said. "Unlike the other forces at the Parkstone." I didn't have time to wonder who she was referring to.

The photo of Lillian graced the photo slider now. Her expression was fierce. Between Lillian, the detectives, and the looky-loo, Mr. Gillrot, I wasn't sure who Mrs. Canterbury was talking about. I was just happy the investigation seemed to be moving along and the residents had yet to threaten to move out, break leases or doors.

That being said, there was still 19 hours to go.

"I'll run up in a couple of minutes and grab the t-shirt," I said. "Then I'll come find you."

"Wonderful!" she said. "You'll be making my day!"

I swapped out the photo of Kip in the courtyard. So sad. I just couldn't take the chance of Bunny seeing it and bursting into tears. It seemed like Parkstone should take such matters into consideration.

Maybe Mrs. Canterbury was right. Maybe I should be in charge.

I grabbed my keys from my purse underneath the concierge's desk. I let Eric know I was running up to my apartment for a couple of seconds.

"Only a couple of seconds?" he said. "I'm not picking you up for a date right now so I'll believe your judgment in time. If you were getting ready for a date, I'd say the run up to your apartment would take a couple of hours."

It's true that my sense of timing could be a bit off, especially when he was picking me up for a date, or he was waiting for me to get ready before we went out. Then, my sense of time was like being in a vacuum. We wouldn't have to worry about this if we lived together like we did when we were in Colorado. It's when he moved out here that he got his own place in Washington, D.C. And when I followed him, I couldn't say no to the discount at the Parkstone and the huge walk-in closet. Eric said he thinks my commitment issues stem from the accident with Hunter. And he might be right. After Hunter's murder, I withdrew from everyone expect Eric and my mom. But Eric didn't come without issues of his own.

He's the one who still hadn't proposed, after 15 years.

"I'm not picking out a cute outfit and getting all dolled up to go on a date with you," I said. "So I'll only be a couple of minutes."

"See you in an hour," he said with a smirk. "Do you want me to cover the concierge desk while you're gone?"

"Really, I'll only be a couple of minutes," I said.

"Beware of the time thief," he said.

I had been late to so many dates which was why I was probably experiencing Eric's chiding. Sometimes I just thought that choosing the perfect DKNY blouse to go with my Lucky jeans and MAC lipstick was worth it.

I made my way through the crowd and to the elevators. Ping! I pressed the tenth floor and headed up to my apartment. The hallway was eerily quiet and I remembered the mysterious footsteps I'd heard in the hallway earlier today.

I put the key in my apartment door lock and turned it. There was something off about the lock. My heart raced faster. I had to turn it twice in order for the door to unlock. It was as if it had been tampered with.

I grabbed a Nike shoe from my closet to prop my door open in case I needed to make a quick escape. I ran to my huge walk-in closet to get the box of t-shirts, grab one and quickly run out.

But the box was gone! Hundreds of "Fore the Cure" neatly folded t-shirts arranged by size were missing. How could this happen? Was there a murderer and a thief at Parkstone? I felt like stomping my feet. It just wasn't fair.

I couldn't believe it. I felt faint. I grabbed onto the doorknob to steady myself. I leaned against the wall accidentally hitting the light switch. The lights went out! I started screaming. I was scaring myself. I fumbled along the wall for the lights and turned them back on as quickly as I could.

Someone had been in my apartment. And someone had stolen the shirts.

I needed to tell Eric right away. Turns out there was a thief at Parkstone, too!

Of course, once I was back in the lobby, I discovered that Eric was interviewing a resident when I needed to talk to him. I started pacing. He was talking to Mr. Graham who was just about the sweetest man I'd ever met. He had been a local news anchor for Fox 5 News until he'd retired a few years ago.

He still made cameos on the news for special anniversary editions and events like that. He'd also purchased a "Fore the Cure" t-shirt because his sister had cancer. Said he'd buy a million t-shirts if he could to help the *cause for the curse*. That's what he called it.

I tried to get Eric's attention, but I didn't want to rush his interview of Mr. Graham, even though I was sure he wasn't worth investigating. He was the nicest guy I knew.

I couldn't wait any longer. I had to tell Eric. For all I knew, the thief could be back at my apartment stealing whatever he or she wanted. What I couldn't understand is that everything else was intact. Only the box of t-shirts was missing.

I walked up to Eric and started waving my arms wildly. "I've been robbed!"

"What?" said Eric. Mr. Graham turned around quizzically.

"Someone stole your purse?" Eric said.

"No, my apartment," I said, the words flowing out of me faster than I could say them.

"Your apartment?" Eric said, looking at me quizzically.

I was hanging on his arm for support. "They stole a box of t-shirts for the charity tournament. It was in my closet and now it's gone."

"Are you sure you didn't bring the box out for any reason and you misplaced it?" he said.

I lowered my voice. "You've seen my apartment," I said. "It's a studio. There's not too many places it could be."

Mr. Graham perked up. "Is that the only thing missing?"

"Yes," I said. "But it's a large box, so it should be easy to find."

"Hold on," Eric said. "We have a murder we're investigating, not a wild goose chase for a box of missing t-shirts."

I couldn't believe it. I was so hurt. Someone stole those t-shirts and they were going to get away with it.

I folded my arms and looked Eric square in the eye. "For all we know that burglary could be linked to the murder. We can't discount it."

"For starters, I'm just glad you're okay," he said.

"Aww," said Mr. Graham until Eric shot him a look.

"That makes two of us," Mr. Graham said.

"Thank you, Mr. Graham. I'm sorry to have interrupted," I said, staring at Eric. "Really, I am. I just think we need to pursue this thief as soon as possible."

"If you'd like I can leak it to the press," Mr. Graham said. "Get the word out there and see if there are any leads."

"That won't be necessary," I said. The last thing Parkstone needed was more bad press. "I'd like to catch this suspect on our own."

"No one has left the building or been let in," Eric said. "So the culprit is among us."

"He could be the same person as the murderer!" I said.

Mr. Graham looked noticeably upset at the thought of a murderer. It would be great if I didn't scare the residents.

"How could they have access to your apartment?" Eric said.

"Well, I'm the only one who has a key," I said which was a slight lie, because Eric also had a key, but I didn't want to say that in front of Mr. Graham. I think Mr. Graham sensed I was holding back because he said, "I'll let you two talk this through. I hope you find whoever stole the shirts."

"Thanks, Mr. Graham," I said. "And if there's anything we can do here at Parkstone to make the next 18 hours a little less miserable, let me know."

Mr. Graham nodded and walked away toward the elevators.

"I wasn't done with that interview," Eric said.

"I didn't mean to scare him away," I said. "You can go back and talk with him if you'd like."

"It's fine," he said. "His alibi panned out. Said he was watching the morning news with his wife. She confirmed. So not much else there I guess." He took a deep breath. "And I'm worried about you."

I was slightly worried about the break-in, too. "You and I are the only people who have a key to my apartment."

"Is there any other way someone could get access to a key?"

After a couple of seconds, it dawned on me. My body felt cold. "There's an extra key to every apartment on the concierge key ring."

He looked me square in the eye. "Where's that?"

"It's behind the concierge desk," I said, knowing that I'd been away from the desk many times. There was ample opportunity for someone to grab the key ring from behind the desk.

Eric motioned for me to follow him. He strutted over to the concierge desk and grabbed the key ring. "It's still here," he said.

I flipped through the key ring and found my apartment key was missing. "So someone still has the key to my apartment," I said. "I won't go back up there. I refuse."

"Listen to me. You don't have to," he said. "I'm going to be keeping an eye on you. If there's anything you need from your apartment, I'll go with you. In the meantime, call a locksmith and get the locks changed."

"Okay," I said, noticing the feebleness in my voice. Who would steal the charity t-shirts? Then I saw Mrs. Canterbury from across the way. I'd have to break the bad news to her, right after I called the locksmith.

CHAPTER 14

The locksmith was on his way and I made myself a cup of Java dark roast coffee to tide me over. A part of me wondered if I was going to be able to make it through the lockdown. The sooner the detectives caught the killer, the better.

I thought about the t-shirts and how I'd have to tell Mrs. Canterbury the bad news, and I was hoping it wouldn't make her feel even more unsettled than she probably already felt.

Then there was Veronica Long, appearing in front of my desk. She was a leisurely golfer who was planning on going to Kip's Congressional golf course "For the Cure" tournament. And she had already pre-paid for a t-shirt, which I now didn't have in my possession to give her.

"About the 'For the Cure,' t-shirt—"

"Keep it," she said.

"What?"

"I'd rather not support such an arrogant golfer," she said. "Nothing to do with the cause, of course."

"Sure," I said, trying unsuccessfully to recline in the uncomfortable concierge chair. "But I don't understand. You signed up for a t-shirt only two weeks ago. And you were going to play in the tournament."

"*Was*," she said. "After Kip accused me of damaging his Mercedes, all bets were off. I don't want any part of the tournament." She looked down at her coffee cup in anguish. Whatever had upset her was still upsetting her.

"Why would he blame you for the damage to his car?"

"Great question," she said. "Maybe because I have the parking spot closest to him. His car was side swiped one night and he blamed me. Of all people!"

"That doesn't make sense."

"It especially doesn't make sense because my car didn't have any scratches on it."

"Okay," I said.

She looked at me intently. "How could I have side swiped his car if my car didn't have any scratches on it?"

"Got it." It sure didn't sound like Veronica had damaged Kip's Mercedes. And I couldn't really understand why he'd think so.

I thought back to whether management had been informed of this incident and was pretty sure it hadn't been reported. There was so much going on at Parkstone. So much I didn't know about. I just couldn't stand it. How could there be so much drama in such a ritzy manor?

Veronica wiped a tear away from her eye. "Look, I've already told the police what happened. And I have an alibi for Kip's murder. I was at breakfast at Café Deluxe this morning, and I have the receipt to prove it."

"I don't doubt you have an alibi," I said. "What's suspicious is who damaged Kip's car and why."

"That's beyond me," she said. "He was always pleasant on the course. And I was going to participate in his "Fore the Cure" golf tournament, but then I realized he wasn't such a great guy when he made those accusations against me."

Geez. Kip had more enemies than I'd originally thought. I believed Veronica when she said she didn't side swipe his car. But if she didn't do it, then who did? And could that individual be the same person who murdered Kip? My head hurt thinking about the mystery and I decided to take a super quick break from behind the concierge desk. After my key had been stolen I didn't think it was a good idea to leave the concierge desk for too long, anyway.

CHAPTER 15

The fax came though at 1:00 p.m. from the main headquarters in New York. It was labeled with the exquisite letterhead and Parkstone emblem featuring two gold crabapple trees with a magnificent line drawing of the Parkstone and the crabapple tree courtyard. It always seemed so grand, that it seemed implicit that whatever was written on it was read by someone privy to lots of official building knowledge.

Dearest Cassie,
We have been informed by detectives on the scene that Mr. Ace was murdered in the crabapple tree courtyard at approximately 8:30 a.m. To the best of our knowledge, you were supposed to be on rounds at that time, walking the crabapple tree courtyard premises to check for anything that might be suspicious or out of place. As these rounds are expected daily, it is my hope that you were so in fact on duty as such.

Please confirm to us at what time the round was conducted. And as to how you didn't discover the body until around 9 o'clock.

We imagine you have an explanation for such occurrences.
Sincerely,
Royce Baxter
Baxter Enterprises

This was going to be a problem. The letter's sentences looked like they were in bold, yelling out to me: Why weren't you on rounds at the correct time? If you were on rounds at the time you were supposed to be, then maybe you could have prevented Kip Ace's murder. I felt weak as a coffee station beverage with cream and sugar.

And I wished more than anything that I had a better explanation for my lack of whereabouts. I had overslept for one. I had stayed up late the night before watching a documentary called the *Low Down on High Fashion*, a behind the scenes look at the world's fashion designers and industry. And I overslept. And then when I got to work I had to field a zillion phone calls about the water being shut down by maintenance, because of a major leak in Apartment 401.

And then there was Bunny. She had called for fashion advice about her brunch outfit. Then about half an hour later, I'd heard a scream and seen a dark shadow among the trees. That's when I knew something was awry.

Now I was sitting at the concierge desk, tormented, thinking that if I could, I would take back my decision to have stayed up late that night, and I'd be out in the courtyard doing my rounds at the regular time. If I'd had done that, Kip's killer would have been caught!

There'd be no 24-hour lockdown. The residents would be happy. Everything would be back to normal.

"Cheer up," Eric said, leaning across the concierge desk.

I snapped out of my reverie. "Cheer up now, or after we find the murderer?" I said.

"Now," he said, "because it could be some time before we find out who killed Kip. And I want to see a smile on your face."

I mustered the closest thing to a smile as I possibly could. I didn't want to seem like a downer, but I couldn't help it. I was sporting a sour attitude with a frown. It's like wearing pink and gray: I don't really want to ever, but sometimes I can't argue they make a good pair.

"I saw you from across the room," he said, "and you looked so depressed."

There's a good reason for that. "It's my fault. If I'd awakened on time and made it downstairs on time to make my rounds, we wouldn't be in this mess."

"The pinpoint murder time doesn't lie, so you may be right," he said. "But you might have walked into whatever happened and not have been able to stop it."

I waved the memo from headquarters around. "I received this memo. Headquarters isn't happy with me."

"Explain what happened," he said.

Eric had the ability to make everything sound like it was going to be okay, whether it was a mistaken food delivery order, or murder mystery misunderstanding. I'd chosen the wrong day to show up late. Now there would just be some more work I'd have to do to make things right.

I thought of it like a hand-sewn dress, versus machine-made. The hand-sewn dress may take more time and work, but it would be more rewarding. All I had to do was make things right.

"You're the best," I said.

"And I think it's great you're manning the concierge desk again. Residents need someone to talk to, and this way no one will be able to steal those keys again."

"No they won't," I said, patting my purse that was hidden under the desk. "Safe and sound."

He smiled and walked away. I typed away on the computer and wrote a memo back to corporate headquarters. "Dear Royce Baxter, I regret to inform you that I was not on time for work the morning of October 10th and, subsequently, was not able to do the daily rounds as usual. I apologize…"

After finishing the memo I placed it in the fax machine and pressed send. I felt responsible for this murder. I had to find out who did it. There was no other way about it.

First things first: I grabbed a diet Snapple Peach Iced Tea—my favorite—from the mini-fridge under the desk. One bottle was only 10 calories. I drank about three a day. At only 10 calories I could indulge and still fit into that tiny black dress for date nights with Eric.

I opened the bottle and read the inside of the cap: "Americans spend more than $630 million a year on golf balls."

I thought about golf and everything it took just to play. There were the shoes, the outfits, the golf clubs, the course membership. It all added up. Playing golf wasn't cheap, neither was donating.

I thought about the charity fundraiser and wondered how much money was going to be missed out on because of the cancellation of the "Fore the Cure" tournament.

Who spent the most money in donations? It was probably one of the course's major players. I decided to get Mrs. Canterbury's attention. She was the charity event's major fundraiser when she wasn't working at the NIH.

She sauntered up to the concierge desk. "Yes, dear," she said. "How are you doing? I see you're stationed at the concierge desk throughout the day. Probably best to have a presence here."

I didn't want to scare her by telling her about the stolen keys. "Do you happen to know who spent the most money for the "Fore the Cure" charity?"

"Dear, I don't know off the top of my head," she said. "There was quite a bit of money donated. But that's all public knowledge. It's available on the tournament's website."

"That's great," I said, re-thinking my fashion career for one in investigating.

"It would be even better if we could actually host the tournament tomorrow," she said. "All that fundraising, for nothing."

"Given the circumstances…" I said.

"I know; it's just that there are some significant donors there," she said. "You'll see."

I typed as quickly as I could until I reached the "Fore the Cure" donor page. I had to catch my breath. "Fifty thousand dollars, from Ginnie, Bunny's best friend?"

"Yes, that sounds right," Mrs. Canterbury said, nodding. She twisted the bracelets on her wrist. All of a sudden she looked uncomfortable.

Why would Ginnie be a big donor at Kip's charity fundraiser? Unless this cause was near and dear to her heart there wasn't a good reason.

Mrs. Canterbury pretended to fan herself nervously. "It's a bit," she said, thinking some more, "a bit odd."

"I would think so," I said.

"I didn't want to think much of it at first," Mrs. Canterbury said. "Mr. Ace is—uh was—such a nice man, and Bunny, just lovely. And of course the more money for the cause, the better."

"But it is suspect," I said. "It's suspect that she would individually donate so much. The other top donors are corporations or well-known celebrities."

"Well, you didn't find out from me," she said. "I didn't think much of it honestly, but in light of everything that's happened…"

I didn't want to involve Mrs. Canterbury much more in the case than she already was. "Don't worry," I said. "The detectives know what they're doing."

"Why yes, best left up to the professionals," she said.

"Exactly, but thank you, Mr. Canterbury," I said. "This is an important fact."

"I did think so myself," she said, clasping her hands together. She rubbed her hands together as if part of a conspiracy.

This was a clue I thought was important to share with Eric.

CHAPTER 16

Sitting at the concierge desk during this mess wasn't as bad as I'd initially thought. In less than 24 hours, the murderer would be caught. The residents would go back to their regularly scheduled lives, and Eric and I would go out on our Sunday date night.

It was just getting to that end-point that was going to be difficult. All that mattered now were clues.

I couldn't believe this new information about Ginnie. Why would she spend all that money to benefit the "Fore the Cure" tournament? I knew she had signed up to get a t-shirt, but I had no idea her contributions were in the thousands. There must be a stronger bond between her and Kip than just Bunny. That's the only thing I could think of to explain such a generous donation.

Judging by Mrs. Canterbury's reaction, she was surprised at Ginnie's dollar amount contribution too. When the lobby cleared out a bit, I'd go ahead and interview Ginnie. I'd need to be discreet about it though, or else I might scare her off.

Just then, a tall figure loomed over me. He had slicked back his brown hair and was wearing a sharp navy blazer and red patterned tie. And then there they were—the teal silk knots! The silk knot cufflinks that I'd lent Mr. Ace a little more than a year ago. It was Mr. Ed Halpern standing in front of me wearing a formidable GLOW watch. And to the best of my knowledge, this was the first appearance he'd made in the lobby since the incident.

"Caught ya napping," he said. He was in an uncharacteristically jovial mood given the circumstances. "How can you get a wink in with all the bustling around you?"

"I wasn't napping," I said. *I was lost in my own reverie trying to think of who had the best motive.*

"Anyway, you're up now," he said.

Mr. Halpern lived on the 12th floor. He, aside from Mr. Ace, was one of the wealthiest men in the building. He was an advertising executive for GLOW watches made famous with their tagline, "What makes you tick?" And they were actually one of Mr. Ace's sponsors.

"My assistant messaged me earlier about what they say happened to Kip," he said. "And well, I didn't believe it. So I turn on the news, and sure enough, the first channel I flip to is news about Parkstone and our beloved Kip."

"It's true," I said. "Your assistant was right. I wish they were wrong though."

Mr. Halpern was late to the game. Really late. There had already been a murder, and a robbery. I thought it ironic that the watch guy was late to the scene, but decided not to point that out. What I wanted to know was how he had the tie knot cuff links I'd loaned Kip.

"Man is that guy going to be missed," he said. "He was one of our proudest sponsor recipients. Brought a lot more in than we were paying out."

There was a popular commercial that had aired for the past couple of weeks of Mr. Ace wearing a GLOW watch golfing on an extravagant golf course. The commercial showed images from morning, noon, and evening with the narrator explaining, "It's always tee time with GLOW watches." It was a great commercial that aired several times a day. It did seem like it was a good partnership.

"That tee time commercial was a classic," Mr. Halpern said. "It resonated with customers in a way our brand hadn't seen in a while."

I decided not to beat around the bush in regards to the silk knots. "How did you get those silk knots from Kip?"

He took a step back. He looked stunned. "How did you know they were from Kip?"

"Because I'm the one who gave them to him," I said. "A little more than a year ago. When he was still alive."

"And that's when he gave them to me. Ran into him in the elevator the other day. He chided me on my tacky dress," he said. "Told me if I was going to be going out to dinner at a fancy restaurant, then I should at least look like I belonged there. Can you imagine that?"

I could. Mr. Ace always seemed very particular about how he dressed.

"He told me to return them to the front desk," he said. "Which I was going to do, but pardon me if I got a bit distracted."

I couldn't fault him for not making that a priority.

"You can have them back," he said, taking them off and sliding them across the concierge desk. "Now, I need to return my assistant's phone calls. Any more questions?"

"Not from me, but the detectives might have some," I said. "They're investigating the murder and interviewing residents floor by floor. They started at the first floor, so you have some time before they get to you."

"Not that I need it," he said shirking his shoulders. "I've got nothing to hide."

I'd learned from Eric that you can't take anyone on their word. Interviewing potential suspects was all about reading in between the lines. My next suspect interview would be with Ginnie. She hadn't left

Bunny's side. Those two were always attached at the hip.

If I could get her away by herself for a second, I could inquire about her generous donations. I noticed there was still some pizza left and I scooped a slice onto a plate and brought it over to Ginnie.

"Going once, going twice," I said.

Ginnie grimaced. "No thank you. That's very sweet of you, but I'm not really in the mood to eat."

Her eyes were red from all the crying, and she held tightly to a crumpled up Kleenex in her right hand.

"Do you have a minute?" I said, trying to be as tactful as possible. She looked at Bunny and said quickly, "I can spare a couple of minutes, but I don't want to leave her for too long."

"I understand," I said. Those too were close on a normal day. I could only imagine she didn't want to leave Bunny's side now.

But Ginnie stepped away, to the winding Chihuly sculpture near the elevators, where we could talk. I thought I'd ease into the questioning. 'As you know, the "Fore A Cure' tournament has been cancelled," I said.

"I assumed as much," she said, "given the circumstances."

"Are you a golf fan?" I said.

She looked perplexed. "Why, yes, sort of," she said. "Why do you ask?"

"It's just that your donation to the tournament was so generous," I said, "and I'd say I could give you a t-shirt, but those aren't available anymore. So you'll be reimbursed for that."

"I'm not worried about the money," she said.

I decided to try a different angle. "Did you have a relative who died of cancer?" I said, trying to figure out why she donated so much money.

"No, I didn't," she said as if I'd ruffled her feathers. "I'm sorry but I don't understand your line of questioning."

"You were the highest donor," I said. "Doesn't that just seem odd?"

She gasped. And she was shaking. "How dare you meddle where you don't belong?" She looked over at Bunny, wrapped up in a blanket. "I have to return to where I'm needed and not answer your silly questions."

That was her decision, but I could still sleuth if I wanted. And something told me if I kept digging, there was a lot to uncover about Ginnie.

CHAPTER 17

Ping! The elevator door opened, and out strutted Anita Halpern, GLOW makeup and design director and wife of the husky Ed Halpern, who had graced me with his presence just moments earlier.

She was wearing a flowing black dress with crocheted sleeves and small embroidered flowers. Her black heels clacked as she bee-lined it to the concierge desk.

"How can I help you?" I said, feeling exhausted and hoping it wasn't going to be too much of a task.

"Kip? Murdered?" she said. "At a place like this?"

She'd heard. "You've heard correctly," I said. "I'm really sorry to have to confirm the bad news for you."

"My husband was the one who told me about it," she said. "But I just had to see for myself. I do not believe it. I turned on the TV, and sure enough, the Parkstone is a murder scene! Cassie, what is going on?"

"If you'd like to discuss the case with the detectives, they're right over there," I said, hoping that maybe she'd want to talk to someone else. I needed time to clear my mind.

"The only thing I know about Kip is his work with GLOW. Which was exquisite," she said. "And he was friends with my husband, thankfully."

Something told me Mr. Halpern didn't have a lot of friends. "The detectives are questioning residents."

"I don't have time now," she said.

"There's a 24-hour lockdown," I said. "Everyone has time. They started on the bottom floors, so you and Mr. Halpern will be some of the last to be interviewed."

"Well, hopefully they'll have caught the murderer by then!"

Anita Halpern turned to walk away when the thought crossed my mind: she hadn't consoled Bunny. Was that suspicious? Considering Mr. Ace was a major athlete representing their brand, I would have thought his widowed wife would be of utmost importance to them. And if her husband Ed Halpern and Kip were such good friends, then I'd at least expect Anita to console Bunny, or offer her condolences. But she didn't even look in her direction. She darted right back toward the elevator and hopped in.

Maybe later she'd say something to Bunny when the crowd thinned out. Or maybe there was something more sinister at play? Eric walked over to the concierge desk and asked, "Who's that?"

Not surprising. Anita was gorgeous. She had long dark hair as shiny as polished crystal. Of course the men would inquire. I just wasn't so thrilled it was my boyfriend doing the inquiring.

"That's Anita Halpern, GLOW advertising executive," I said. "Married to Ed Halpern." I wanted to make it clear she was off the market.

"She looks familiar," Eric said.

"She's active in golf, but really is best known for her status at GLOW," I said. "Not that those execs are usually famous."

He smirked. "It's not that." He thought about it some more. "The commercials!" He pounded his fist on the concierge desk. A few heads turned to see what all the commotion was about.

"Oh right," I said, remembering a commercial from a couple months back featuring both Anita and Kip.

"Anytime is a good time to GLOW," I said, repeating one of the more memorable lines from the commercial.

"That's it!" Eric said. "That's where I know her from."

I was glad we'd cleared that up. I didn't want to spend too much time listening to Eric talk about Anita Halpern. Although as I got to thinking about her, I did think it was odd that she'd been in that commercial with Kip. While she was pretty enough to be a model (maybe even a runway model given her height), she was by no means an actress by profession. At GLOW she was the director of hair and makeup. So why was she acting in a two-minute GLOW commercial with Kip?

This was something I'd need to investigate. Anita Halpern was reserved, but I'd find a way to crack her quips.

CHAPTER 18

Things seemed to quiet down as the detectives interviewed some residents in the far part of the lobby. Then I heard the sound of the fax machine. Correspondence from corporate headquarters!

I couldn't wait to read what it said. That enthusiasm changed right after I read the memo:

Dearest Cassie,

We regret to inform you that the detectives have notified us that Kip's time of death was 8:30 a.m. Since this is the time you were supposed to be doing rounds, we are led to believe that you were late for such tasks.

Due to this revelation, please understand why we are asking for your resignation after the mandatory 24 hours is up. You have been a stellar employee up until this point. Please understand, we have a level of competence that needs to be upheld so that everything at Parkstone runs smoothly and the residents are cared for. Any disregard for that standard will not be accepted lightly.

We're sorry to have to let you go.

Sincerely,

Royce Baxter, Baxter Enterprises

I was reading the fax when all of a sudden I heard a blood curdling scream from the leasing office. Jet-Setter arched his back and the fur ball's hair spiked out like a fan. I dropped the fax I was reading and headed over in panic to the leasing office. There she was. Leaning against her cane near the window. She tapped her cane twice on the floor before speaking. "I can't find it," she said. "It's missing."

"What?" I said, thankful to see she was okay. Jet-Setter ran circles around my feet with all of the excitement.

"*Their* lease," she said.

"Whose lease?" I said, unable to follow her train of thinking.

"Mr. and Mrs. Ace's lease!" she said, practically pulling her hair out with the hand that wasn't holding onto the cane.

At this point, many residents and a few detectives from the lobby had appeared in the leasing office entranceway. "There's nothing to see here," I said. "Lillian was just startled, but it's been resolved now."

Eric stayed back while he shooed away the other detectives and residents who trickled back to the lobby.

"Is everything okay in here?" Eric said.

"Yes and no," Lillian said. "I'm fine, but there's been stolen property—the lease of Mr. and Mrs. Ace!"

"Who would steal that, and why?" I said as Jet-Setter landed, plopping down right on top of my Jimmy Choo fluffy slippers I'd grabbed earlier from my apartment.

"I don't know," she said.

"And it's definitely stolen, not misplaced?" Eric said.

Lillian looked defiant. "Look at how impeccable this office is. I keep it that way so that when I want a lease, it's at my fingertips."

I looked around the office. It was super organized. And that wasn't anything new. It had been that way since Lillian had started with the company five years ago.

"Maybe whoever stole the lease also stole the tournament t-shirts?" I said.

"Motive is key," said Eric. "Once you open the motive door, you'll find the culprit on the other side."

"There's no motive for stealing a lease," Lillian said, raising her arms and cane in exasperation.

"Unless of course, it's someone who didn't want the Aces to renew their lease and keep renting here," I said.

"They had already stayed at Parkstone longer than they had expected," she said.

Eric crossed his arms. "Why is that?"

"Because Kip wanted to. He loved it here at the Parkstone," she said. Just hearing those words made me happy for Kip. At least he was where he wanted to be during his final hours.

Lillian started shaking her head. She lowered her voice. "But Mrs. Ace didn't want to renew. She would've been happy as a hen to leave here. Couldn't get out soon enough."

Eric furrowed his brow. "From what I've gathered, the Aces were living at Parkstone because their house was damaged from a lightning strike, correct?"

"Yes," I said. "And they chose Parkstone, not only because of all the wonderful amenities, but because Bunny's best friend Ginnie lives here, too."

Lillian perked up. "So why wouldn't Mrs. Ace want to live here near her best friend?"

"Good question," Eric said, rubbing his chin. "Why wouldn't she?"

It seemed to me that not all was gloss and empire waist dresses when it came to Bunny and Ginnie's friendship. There was tension between them that could have resulted in a stolen lease and possibly murder. Jet-Setter arched his back and walked toward the door. A good reminder I would have to get back to the concierge desk.

Lillian sat back down at her desk with a loud humph. As Eric and I were walking out, he said, "So as not to worry the residents, I'm going to announce that we found the lease. If I find the culprit, you'll be the first to know."

I had already narrowed down the suspects in my head. An angry resident (including Ginnie) who didn't want the Aces renewing their lease, or maybe it was Mrs. Ace herself.

Eric hung around the concierge desk. And then finally he said, "This isn't easy to say, but I have something to tell you."

Did he want to break up? Did he know who the murderer was? His smoldering eyes were now glum. I had a lump in my throat. "Go ahead," I said. "What is it?"

"There haven't been any leads on the case so far, and as of now, you're the lead suspect," he said, frowning. "I'm really sorry, not much I can do about it. You were the first one on the scene. And your bracelet was found at the scene."

My bracelet! I knew something was missing. "How did you find it?"

"Your bracelet was found right next to Kip."

"It must have fallen off when I knelt down to check his pulse," I said. "I was holding the cats, too, to keep them from getting too close to the body, so it must have slipped off." I remembered my gold 'C' initial charm bracelet.

"I know that," he said. "I believe you. It's just that the other guys don't."

"Well, what about motive," I said. "I have no motive to kill him."

"That's the only reason you're not at the station," he said. "I hope we find one or think of one that matches another suspect. I can't say for sure you won't be hauled in."

Hauled in? There's no way that's going to happen. I had to solve this mystery as soon as possible! "I'm going to solve this mystery," I said. "And I'm going to prove I'm innocent and that I'm a great concierge at Parkstone. Are you going to help?"

"Of course," he said. "Whatever you want. And if this is wrapped up by tomorrow tonight, I'm still on for dinner."

"Then we have a mystery to solve," I said, squeezing his hand. "Let me know what you find out, and I'll do the same."

He looked at me with his smoldering eyes that were dark brown and sexy. "You got it."

I took the fax from headquarters and folded it into my pocket. I'd write back to them later, after I'd solved the murder. There were still so many things to investigate: the Aces' scratched Mercedes, why Anita was featured in the GLOW commercial with Kip, the extra Fitbit steps, the shouting voices between a woman and Kip that were heard this morning, and the argument I had overheard between Rich Gibbons and Kip a couple of weeks ago. There was also the mystery of the missing lease, which could be somehow linked to the murder, and the missing t-shirts.

I had to work fast. I had less than 24 hours to clear my name. *And* I wanted my bracelet back.

CHAPTER 19

It crossed my mind that nobody believed in me. They all thought I was a joke, just a pragmatic concierge who liked stylish manicures and throwing parties for the residents in the club room.

Was I any better than that? Could I prove myself? My breath quickened at the thought of being taken seriously. If I could, a weight would be lifted off my shoulders. This had been my first real job besides retail and administrative work, and I'd been given a lot of responsibility.

If I couldn't do this, people would lose what little faith they had in me. And worse yet, I'd lose faith in myself.

What am I good at? I'm good at attention to detail. Like being able to spot designer clothes on residents. Or observing their elegant handwriting when they sign for a package. Or picking up on their cool initials like GAL for Ginnie Abigail Langford.

Whether they knew it or not, these residents depended on me. And for more than just cuff links and dollies. My best shot at making something of myself would be to use my attention to detail skills toward the investigation. And help the lives of all the residents by solving the crime. One detail after the next.

It occurred to me that there was a worst and best case scenario. Best case, they saw me as competent. Worst case, they saw me as an incompetent concierge who'd murdered the beloved Kip Ace!

Solving the crime was becoming a must, like dangling pearl earrings with a sweetheart neckline.

CHAPTER 20

I debated whether to disassemble the coffee machine. Residents might want caffeine, and I could use another cup of dark roast to stay awake. I hadn't planned on working a double shift. But I was up for it. I had to be.

There were rumblings from the detectives who sat huddled near the far lobby entrance—the one next to the courtyard. I'd checked the surveillance video, but there wasn't footage of anyone but Kip walking out to the courtyard at that time. So any resident who walked out there must have taken the stairs.

Kip would always prop the courtyard door open when he went out, so that would explain why they didn't need their FOB to get back inside once they were in the courtyard. Just then, the elevator door opened. It was the programmer, Rich Gibbons.

Now was my chance.

He nodded hello to me and walked over to the coffee machine. Most likely he was going for a barista blend, his usual. There were so many buttons on that machine, you'd think it would take a programmer to figure it out. But he pressed on the buttons with huffy agitation. The machine sputtered and he placed a cup underneath the spout.

He looked more agitated than usual. He twitched a bit and shook his head. Was he becoming overridden with guilt for killing Kip?

I didn't mean to jump to conclusions. But it was difficult not to. He'd had an argument with Kip recently. And this mystery had to be solved within 24 hours. The sooner I started questioning, the better!

As Rich waited patiently for his coffee, I asked myself, could he be that cold-hearted? I thought the answer was no, but only an interrogation would tell.

In the time it took him to make his coffee, I'd thought of a way to approach him without seeming confrontational. He took his coffee from the machine and took a seat at the near lobby entrance.

His boxy, stout figure contrasted with the plush chairs' high backs. "Mind if I join you?" I said.

"I wouldn't mind the company," he said.

"This has been a long day, for everyone, especially someone as close to Kip as you."

"Frenemies," he said. "That's what I'd call it. He was a genius, and I fear I fell short in his eyes."

Genius? I doubt that would be a word used to describe a frenemy. Seemed like he highly regarded Kip. "You were working on a project together, right?" I said holding my breath. I was going out on a limb here. That was information gleaned from a conversation I'd overheard two weeks ago in the lobby.

"It was a business venture," he said. "Didn't quite get off the ground." He took a sip of coffee.

My eyebrows perked up. He continued. "It was an app if you must know. Kip and I were working together on creating an app to perfect a golfer's swing."

"That sounds exciting!" I said, totally surprised. Surprised first of all that he was divulging so much information and, secondly, that they were working together on creating an app.

"Would've been exciting if we could have just agreed on something—the interface, the pricing, the marketing. We delayed it so long because of disagreements, that it just caved."

"And now..." I said.

"And now it's too late," he said glaring. His eyebrows, usually full and nicely arched were now furrowed.

"Are you a golf player yourself?" I asked.

"Tried my hand at it once or twice," he said. "Got a set of clubs, but every time I go to take a swing, I feel like a bumbling computer ape who wishes he could swing a nine iron."

So, the computer programmer had a motive *and* the murder weapon. "Are you still going to launch the app even though he's dead?"

"I thought about it. Just doesn't seem right without him. On the other hand, I put a lot of work into developing the technology and now it's just going to waste."

"That would be a pity," I said. "So, what are you thinking?"

"The answer is: I don't know. Thought about launching it and naming it after him. Like name it Ace." He was looking up at me as if testing to see if I liked the name. "I don't know."

The computer programmer was sounding more and more like an indecisive, torn-apart friend than an enemy, let alone murderer.

"I think it's a good idea."

Then the programmer seemed to start getting upset again. "I mean, why should my idea suffer because someone killed him?"

"Good point," I said. "Just maybe think about it like this: Is it still a viable idea without him?"

"That's a good way to think about it," he said. "Thanks, Cassie, that was really helpful."

Helpful! Wow. I'd already done better than I'd initially thought I would. I'd approached the programmer, and he'd told me the important details. Was I missing anything?

Not that I could think of right now. But if I did think of something, I knew where to find him—Apt. 427, where he'd most likely be sitting in front of his computer.

I made myself another dark roast and settled in behind the concierge desk. I knew it would be just a matter of minutes before a resident submitted another request: broken dishwasher, smelly garbage disposal, closet door not closing. In fact, I was so distraught with negatives that I had almost forgotten that they'd turned the water back on. One less thing to worry about.

Ping! The elevator door opened and out walked my friend Ben Harrison.

My head felt light. He looked dashing in his olive-green pants and black button down shirt. He was carrying a video camera bag that was slung over his shoulder. His smiled at me and then glanced in the direction of the detectives.

Eric sat there talking with residents. My heart belonged to Eric, but I'd always thought my friend Ben Harrison was sensible.

"Can I steal you away for a minute or two?" he said.

"Or three or four," I said, hopeful to have a reason to leave the lobby.

He smiled.

He lowered his voice. "I have something to show you," he said. "It's important. Stop by."

"You got it," I said. I finished my coffee, feeling re-energized by the caffeine. When I was sure the detectives were occupied with talking about the case, I slipped up the stairs to Ben Harrison's apartment. It was a nice one bedroom overlooking the courtyard.

"So glad you're here," he said, opening the front door and ushering me in. "I can't believe I found this, and I don't know what to do about it."

Oh no. He needed advice. This would test my advice skills again.

"Advice about what?"

"This," he said. He pressed play on the TV. We watched as a beautiful time lapse video appeared on the screen. The video was of the courtyard. The courtyard at Parkstone!

"Why, I think that's really beautiful if you ask my opinion," I said, nervous that this was maybe going to be an important clue to the case.

"Just wait for it," he said.

Then all of a sudden, the sky got lighter. Lighter shades of red and purple and then there it was: a metal stick flying through the air and landing in the middle of the courtyard.

"Oh my God," I said. "Is that the murder weapon? How horrible."

"It looks like a golf club if you ask me," he said.

"Or a cane!" I said.

"A cane?" he said. "Why? Who has a cane?"

There went me and my big mouth. I had been thinking that maybe it was Lillian.

"Hmmm," he said, "who has a cane? Lillian, the leasing agent?"

"Shhhhh," I said. "It was just an idea. She can be mean. I've seen her act like a pit bull when provoked. And I checked when Kip Ace's lease was up and it was up this month. That means Lillian was doing her best to make sure Kip was signing again and paying an increase. My guess is he wasn't too happy about that."

There was still the case of the missing lease that had yet to be solved.

"That's not a bad theory," he said. "I just wanted to make sure you saw the time lapse video. Just happened I've been making these a couple days a week for a documentary filmmaking class at George Mason."

"I'm glad you showed me," I said. I had made myself honorary sleuth in this case, so the more evidence the better. "What time was that filmed?"

"According to the footage, around eight this morning," he said.

"Are you going to show the detectives?"

"What do you think?" he said. "That's what I'd like your opinion about."

Why was everyone asking my advice about everything? Time again to step up to the plate. "I would eventually," I said. "It can't hurt."

He looked hesitant. "I don't want to get anyone in trouble."

"Listen, let me see what I can do first, and then give them the evidence as a last resort?"

"That sounds like a plan," he said.

"One more thing," I said. "Since we see the weapon falling through the sky, does that mean that someone on a floor above you tossed the golf club through the air and it hit Kip and that's how he was murdered? And if so, was it intentional or accidental?"

He shrugged. "That's where the sleuthing comes into play I guess," he said. "So what clues have you put together so far?"

I was so glad he asked.

CHAPTER 21

Laughter erupted from where the detectives were stationed at the far end of the lobby near the courtyard exit. I don't think they'd even noticed I was gone.

"Aliens," said Detective Williams. "That's my best guess. Seriously, guys, what left these holes?"

I looked at the clock. It was 1:45 a.m. If the cops weren't taking the murder seriously, then it was up to me. I had around seven hours left to solve the mystery. If I or the cops couldn't solve the mystery within that timeframe, one murderous resident might go free.

"What do you want from us?" said the other detective. "It looks like alien marks on the ground. I don't know what to make of those round spots in the grass."

They held up pictures of the courtyard grass which they were examining. I knew I had one picture of the holes on my phone. What had caused the circles in the grass near Kip's body?

I remembered how those circles looked on the grass when I'd found Kip. They were about two inches in diameter. Really bizarre. I thought it was safe to rule out alien marks, but what could have made them?

Ping! The elevator door opened. And Lillian walked out, cane first. There was Lillian's cane, whack! Right onto the marble floor. Then Lillian emerged. As slowly as the elevator door closed, the answer hit me. Lillian's cane. That's what made the hole marks!

I stared at her cane. The rubber bottom of it was about two inches in diameter. That's it! My joy at discovering the answer turned to fear as she approached me with a stern face. I could be facing a murderer!

"Would you like a cup of coffee or tea?" I said, graciously rising to the occasion.

"I'm capable of making it myself," she said. "I have an important question to ask you, Cassie."

And then without knowing what else to say, I said, "Same."

We walked into Lillian's pristine leasing office, and with each thud of her cane I kept thinking about Kip's corpse surrounded by those circles on the lawn. Could she have been the one to murder Kip? The motive could be an argument over the lease. It's still odd that the lease was stolen.

And there was the noise complaint from this morning. That could have been Lillian! My mind was racing with thoughts about Lillian being the murderer when she said, "So was it you?"

She was looking me dead in the eyes. It made me so uncomfortable I got a lump in my throat. I swallowed loudly. "Was it me what?"

"Did you steal the lease?"

"Oh," I said startled. Enough with the lease already. "No, it wasn't. I'd have no need to do that. And I have no idea where it is."

"You didn't just steal it to mess with me?" she said. "You'd do that."

Now she was pointing her cane at me. I stepped back for comfort. She moved forward.

She continued to talk with her cane pressed against the wall next to my face. "We never really did get along," she said. Then thud! Her cane hit the floor right in front of my cushy slippers. Jet-Setter, who was by my side, squealed and jumped on top of the desk, curling up on top of a pile of papers.

"We get along well enough," I said. "I always thought so."

She inched forward more, her long dark hair and disbelieving eyes menacing. "I'm not sure you think much of anything. Sure, you're happy to have your concierge job, but you're just a fashion-conscience female who sits at the concierge desk and half the time shows up late for work."

Wow. It took me a second. If I digested all those negatives, I'd need a bigger size Yves Saint Laurent wrap dress.

"That's a lot," I said.

"I could continue."

How evil and uncalled for. Two could play this game. I reminded myself I could be in a room with a murderer, so I shouldn't hold back. "I know you were out in the courtyard talking with Kip before he was murdered."

She gasped. I stepped forward. She and her cane took one step back. Jet-Setter perked up like he was watching a game of tennis and was following where the ball landed.

"Your cane made the indentations in the grass around Kip's body."

"I can explain," she said.

"I'm not finished," I said. The ball was in my court. Eric always said to back the suspect into a wall first. Then deliver a wallop. "There's a noise complaint from this morning regarding a man—Kip, I believe—and a woman—who I believe was you—arguing in the courtyard."

She gasped again. Now it was time to deliver the wallop. "I could be nice about this. But I'm not going to be. I'm going to tell the detectives you were in a heated argument with Kip during the time of his murder. And *you* don't have an alibi."

"I was in my office, working," she said.

"Who can vouch for you?" I said walking away.

She whacked her cane on the ground. "Wait!" she cried. "I can explain."

I turned around and with as much tenacity as I could muster said, "Explain it to the detectives."

With that, Jet-Setter plopped down from the desk, kicking up the pile of papers with his right paw. They scattered everywhere across the table and the floor.

If there's one thing Lillian hated, it was a mess.

CHAPTER 22

I was trying my very best to overhear what Lillian was saying to the detectives over the low mumble of voices in the lobby. Eric kept avoiding my eyes. Why wouldn't he give me some hint about how it was going?

I told him the circle marks were from Lillian's cane and about the noise complaint. The only thing that didn't really fit was the cane, or whatever the object was in Ben Harrison's time lapse video which looked more like a golf club than a cane. And if Lillian was in the courtyard yelling at Kip, how could her cane be falling through the air?

Was it instead a flying golf club that was the murder weapon? Is that what whacked Mr. Ace in the head leaving him to die?

Lost in my reverie, I only snapped out of it because Jet-Setter was clawing at my legs. He was hungry. I filled up his food bowl and took a seat back at the concierge desk. I was trying to read Eric and Lillian's body language. Then I heard a familiar shrill and comforting voice, "My dear Cassie! I have pie," she said.

Mrs. Canterbury was the best. She was always so bright and cheery, and she was wearing the Ralph Lauren frilly floral blouse I'd picked out for her at the beginning of the season. It looked great with the white jeans and white leather braided belt.

"It's blueberry pie," she said. "Just happened to have all the ingredients, and thought, well, why not?"

"You are the best," I said, hopping off my concierge chair.

"There's more upstairs, too," she said. "Thought you should get the first piece."

"You are so thoughtful, Mrs. Canterbury," I said. I remembered back to my first day starting my concierge job and Mrs. Canterbury had been the most welcoming resident. She brought me a gift basket with dried apricots, iced tea, granola bars, yogurt and daisies.

It was the perfect welcoming gift. The thing with being the concierge is that I have to be at the desk 24/7. This way I didn't go hungry.

"Here," she said, dishing up another slice on a plate. "Take a piece for that detective friend of yours."

Mrs. Canterbury was shrewd.

"You noticed?"

"How could I not?" she said. "The way he looks at you. Completely in love."

That's why I couldn't understand why he hadn't proposed to me yet. Mrs. Canterbury placed the plate of pie oozing with blueberries next to mine on the counter. "Now, neither of you will go hungry."

"Thank you," I said, relieved for her kindness. "And how are you doing in all of this?"

"Oh me," she said, placing her hand over her heart. "I'm hanging in there."

"Is there anything I can do to make this situation more…pleasant?"

"Oh, dear," she said clutching the pie dish, "These are unfortunate circumstances. Kip, Kip was quite an idol."

I thought about how I'd found him dead this morning. The cool air breezing by my skin as I trucked up the hill to find shadows from the sunflowers moving over Kip's body.

She continued. "His death has cast a shadow on Parkstone," she said. "A dark, dark shadow."

"Have you spoken with the detectives yet?" I said between bites of blueberry pie.

"I have," she said. "Gave them my alibi. My morning whereabouts. They were lovely. I do hope they find the murderer. And fast!" She clenched her fist.

"Me, too," I said, thinking I might find out who did it before they did. But I didn't want to worry Mrs. Canterbury with such matters.

She smiled. "Stay strong. And remember to share that other piece with the detective."

I laughed. Mrs. Canterbury thinking I'd steal the other piece for myself was hilarious. I'd save the slice for Eric and give it to him just as soon as he finished talking with Lillian.

What could they be talking about anyway? What could be taking so long?

If Lillian was guilty, it would be a case closed by now. She had a motive and she was on the scene of the crime at the time the murder was committed. What more could a detective ask for in a suspect?

Just then Jet-Setter purred against my leg and meowed. I picked him up and gave him a hug. Even the house cat was keen on finding out the lowdown.

CHAPTER 23

Eric and Lillian were finally done talking. I waved frantically to get Eric's attention to come over to the concierge desk to see me and pick up his plate of homemade blueberry pie.

"What do we have here?" he said, grinning ear-to-ear. Lillian must not be the suspect or else he wouldn't be so happy.

"Blueberry pie courtesy of Mrs. Canterbury," I said. "And p.s., she's on to us."

He smiled. "I guess our chemistry is undeniable?"

"Yes," I said, leaning across the desk. "We can't talk our way out of that one."

He looked up from the plate of blueberry pie. "You really got this detective lingo down, don't you?"

"Speaking of detective work," I said. "Why aren't you reading Lillian her Miranda rights and hauling her to the station?"

"Because she has an airtight alibi," he said.

"Since when?" I said. "Ten minutes ago? She told me she was in her office doing work."

"And she was," he said. "The doorman confirmed it."

"But the heated argument with Kip," I said. "That's proof!"

"It's proof they disagreed about the lease," he said. "And that's about it. The doorman saw her return to her office after being in the courtyard, which she said is where she and Kip had a heated argument about the lease. The doorman also remembers seeing Kip walking around the courtyard *after* that argument when Lillian was in her office doing work."

"She has an alibi," I said, throwing up my arms.

"Worse things have happened," he said.

I knew that was true, but I wanted my work enemy to be the murderer. It just seemed to fit.

"At least we crossed one more suspect off the list," he said.

A list! That was a great idea. That's what I should do. I'd write a list of all the suspects and then cross them off once I learned they did or did not have an airtight alibi until I narrowed it down to one murder suspect.

I must have been lost in my own daydreaming because Eric said, "Cassie, are you okay? Are you paying attention?"

"I'm fine," I said. "Really. Just becoming consumed with solving this mystery."

He squeezed my hand. "Don't get too wrapped up in it," he said. "That's what we're here for."

He looked so handsome in his suit. "I know," I said. "But it's difficult not to get wrapped up in it. We're not allowed to leave Parkstone, and one of us is a murderer. What else is there to consume my time?"

"Yes, I understand," he said. "But you don't have to get so wrapped up in it that you lose focus of other things, too."

Jet-Setter, with a squeal, pounced on top of the counter. He plopped on top of our clasped hands and purred. Jet-Setter was always there to lighten the mood between us.

"I'm going to go back to interviewing residents," he said. "I'll let you know if there are any leads."

"Yes, any update that involves a main suspect beside myself would be great."

"We'll solve this," he said giving me a peck on the cheek.

Jet-Setter clawed at the desk. I wasn't feeling too confident in their investigation either.

CHAPTER 24

I decided to make a suspect list. At the top of that list was Rich Gibbons. He and Kip had been overheard arguing just weeks before the murder. Fighting over their business deal could have led to the murder, and as far as I knew now, he didn't have an alibi.

Then there was Bunny Ace, Kip's wife. I didn't want to add her to the list, but thought I had to in the interest of being thorough. Their marriage seemed perfect from the outside, but could have been a mess on the other side—like an embroidered hanky. And for proof there was the angry *National Inquirer* picture. Alibi: unclear.

Then there was Ginnie Paige, Bunny's best friend, who seemed to be a good friend of both Kip and Bunny. An argument could have turned nasty and Kip could have wound up dead. Alibi: unclear.

Next up to the suspect list were Ed and Anita Halpern, the top GLOW executives who had befriended Kip and had worked with him as well. It seemed as if Ed wasn't too happy that Anita had had to step in as the actress beside Kip. Alibi: unclear.

Then there was Mr. Gillrot. On a good day, he was nasty, bitter and snide. On a bad day, he was glued to the concierge desk ranting about residents or politics or building management. He wasn't one to hold back. Kip and Mr. Gillrot had gotten into spats here and there. One of those spats could have escalated and wound up in death. Alibi: unclear.

I'd need to get actual alibis from residents, or prod Eric for the alibis if he already had them. The list was as follows:

Rich Gibbons

Bunny Ace

Ginnie Paige

Ed and Anita Halpern

Mr. Gillrot

It was a comprehensive list. And I couldn't believe that someone on this list was likely the murderer.

From my perch at the concierge desk, I spotted Rich Gibbons typing at his laptop at the far end of the lobby. He was pounding away at the keys with fury. Was he still working on the app business? I needed to find out his alibi for this morning.

I walked over and sat down in the chair next to him, picking up a magazine off the table. "How's it going?" I said, trying to sound casual and non-threatening.

"Kind of busy here," he said. "The Internet in my apartment is spotty, so I decided to work from the lobby."

"Great idea," I said.

"What's the Parkstone's wifi password?" he said.

"It's the word *luxury* and the address 7620," I said.

"Got it, thanks." He typed even more furiously at the keyboard if that was humanly possible.

"Make any decisions about the app?" I said, thumbing through the magazine as a ruse.

"No, not yet," he said. "Don't expect to for some time." He paused. "Why? Do you golf?"

"Not really," I said. "Just interested in apps. Always looking for a new one to download."

He nodded.

I continued. "What was going to be your share of the earnings from the app?"

"What?!" he said. "That's an inappropriate question."

Could this mean there might be a reason for the programmer to off Kip to get a greater share of the earnings? Just when I thought things were going well and that I'd become better at sleuthing, I go and ask a question like that. Who does that?

I was not making a good sleuth. I looked around at the ornate wall décor of the Parkstone. If I was meant to be here I had to be a good sleuth. And part of being a good sleuth was asking the right questions.

The programmer's face crinkled up. "I'm not giving you a second more of my time."

"I'm very sorry," I said. "It's just that there's been a murder at Parkstone, and we're all—"

"Leave it up to the detectives," he said. "They've already interrogated me. And I've told them what I know. I don't need a fraud like you to interrogate me."

I was about to ask a question to get his alibi and then he said, "You're the concierge the last time I checked. I shouldn't have confided in you in the first place."

"Your Ace app idea is safe with me," I said, meaning it. Another part of me was hoping he wasn't a killer, one that was going to get off scott free while Kip would never play a game of golf again.

CHAPTER 25

I thought it might be a good idea to get a workout in. It would give me time to mull over the murder mystery and blow off some steam. I'd let Eric know where I was going to be so he wouldn't worry when he didn't see me at the concierge desk.

"Do you want me to go with you?" he said. "I don't think it's safe for you to go alone."

"I'll be fine," I said somewhat rattled that Eric thought I needed an escort to my apartment. "Well, on second thought."

"Just let me tell the guys I'll be right back," he said.

In the elevator, I decided to ask about the alibis of some of the suspects on my list. "Rich Gibbons," I said.

"He didn't do it," he said. "One, he's too brainy and second he has an airtight alibi: he was playing computer games at 8:30 a.m. That time is stamped on his computer."

"Oh," I said, disappointed that I'd have to cross off the number one suspect on my list.

"Try again," he said. "We're trying to interview the suspects as quickly as we can, but in a building with this many residents, it could take a while."

Ping! The elevator door opened and we walked out. "Just as long as I know you're safe," he said. Jet-Setter and Cashmere raced ahead to my apartment door. We smiled.

I ran in quickly and changed into my stretch pants and tank top. I still couldn't believe that someone had broken into my apartment and stolen an entire box of the golf charity fundraiser t-shirts. I was wishing I had one left to wear to the gym.

I scooped up Jet-Setter and Cashmere who'd already settled in and headed out the door into the hallway, where Eric leaned against the wall flipping through his notebook. "I shouldn't be sharing this with you," he said, "because it's confidential information, but the main people who don't have an alibi—an airtight alibi, that is—are the Halperns."

I gasped. Seriously? Everything about their perfect life seemed as airtight as a Ziploc bag.

He continued. "Their alibis are themselves. They're each vouching for each other," he said. "That's never airtight."

"I spoke with them briefly," I said. "You know they did business with Kip."

"The GLOW commercial?" he said.

I nodded.

"Yeah, they mentioned that," he said. "Didn't seem to go too well."

"I can't see either of them being a murderer though," I said. Anita looked killer in her stilettos, but that was about it.

"Besides you, they're definite persons of interest."

The thought that I was still a person of interest made a lump form in my stomach. My breathing quickened and I had to assure myself that I could prove I was innocent. I would find whoever did this. And if it was the Halperns, then so be it.

We headed up to the gym where I said goodbye to Eric, promising him I'd be back in the lobby in half an hour, and for him not to worry about me.

When I opened the gym door, it was just as I'd suspected. I'd have the gym all to myself in the wee hours of the morning. Most likely, everyone else was spending the lockdown in their apartments, watching

TV, talking on the phone, relaxing out on their balconies.

I worked out on the elliptical for 30 minutes and barely broke a sweat. I couldn't help but think about the mystery and try to figure out motive and alibis. It made my knees weak.

I decided to wipe down the elliptical, then wash my face and neck in the locker room. When I walked by the sauna I realized I wasn't alone.

The sauna emitted a warm orange glow. The light was visible from inside the women's locker room. Who else was here? I picked up a towel from the stack near the lockers. I figured I could possibly use it to defend myself if needed. Wrapping a killer up in a towel could be my modus operandi.

I gingerly rounded the corner, towel clenched. I stood in front of the sauna to see Anita Halpern wearing a bikini, soaking in the sauna's heat. She had cucumbers placed over her eyes and there was what looked to be an unread *Glamour* magazine on the bench next to her. Not a bad way to decompress.

I decided I could pass the time for a while, and investigate. I knocked on the sauna door.

Anita jumped, the cucumbers flying off her eyes and onto the floor. I opened the wooden door, "It's me," I said. "Cassie."

"You. Scared. Me," she said. "I'm here to relax, not be startled out of my wits."

"Don't mind me," I said, taking a seat next to her on the bench. "I can only stay about five minutes. We're very busy at the concierge desk."

"Stay as long as you want," she said. "The temperature is at a relaxing 80 degrees Celsius."

"This is much more relaxing than being at the concierge desk," I said, noticing that beads of sweat were already forming on my neck. I used the towel to dab them off. I wasn't sure how long I was going to last.

"How is everything in the lobby?" she said, placing the cucumbers back over her eyes and tilting her head against the wooden sauna wall.

"Hectic," I said. "Very hectic. You have the right idea by camping out in here."

"I've only been here for the past hour," she said with a smirk. "I needed some escape."

Well, this was as good an idea as any. Anita always looked put together. Like she was in charge of every aspect of her life, from her career at GLOW to her bouffant hair and perfectly manicured nails.

"The lobby is such a zoo right now, I decided I could take a few minutes to unwind before returning to battle the crowds," I said.

"Is *she* still there?" Anita asked.

"Who?"

"The Parkstone Piranha," she said.

I burst out laughing. "Who's that?"

Anita lifted a cucumber from her right eye. "Ginnie Langford."

I laughed again. "Why would you call Ginnie Langford a piranha?"

"Oh dear, there's so much you don't know."

Apparently. Ginnie Langford seemed like one of the nicest ladies I'd ever met. She always said hi and bye to me when walking through the lobby, she had donated thousands of dollars to the "Fore the Cure" charity tournament, and she was a true-blue friend to Bunny Ace.

"What about her don't I know?" I said not sure I really wanted to know. But if it would get me one step closer to solving the crime, then it'd be worth it.

"Why she and Mr. Ace have been having an affair for about a year now," she said.

"What?" I said, waving my arms, not knowing what to do. All of a sudden I'd forgotten about the hot temperature of the sauna and my drying out skin. The real heat was an affair between Kip Ace and his wife's best friend. "How do you know this?"

"Evvvvveryyyyone knows this," she said.

There was a long pause. She must have known I was still in disbelief so she repeated, "Everyone."

"Even Bunny?" I said, not being able to picture her condoning such behavior.

"Good point," she said adjusting her head along the wall. "Everyone but Bunny. I mean, do you think she'd still be friends with Ginnie if she knew?"

This changed everything. It changed how I felt about Kip—my childhood golf idol who I was now learning was quite complex. And this changed the murder mystery. One suspect, Ginnie, potentially had a really strong motive. Especially if Kip had decided he no longer wanted to have an affair with her. A murder of unrequited love?

"Are you sure Kip wanted to continue it?" I said.

"He's been two-timing Bunny ever since I've known him," she said. "We met about a year ago on the set of the GLOW commercials. I had to stand in as the actress because nobody wanted to act alongside him."

"But what if he had a change of heart?" I said.

She tapped her manicured nails on the wooden bench. "Or she? She also could have had a change of heart." She paused. "Although I doubt it. Usually good looking, millionaire athletes aren't easy to let go."

So if anyone was going to break it off, it would have been Kip, Anita was suggesting. And that's a powerful motive for Ginnie to have committed murder. I had to get out of there and go back to the lobby to investigate. Ginnie was probably still there. She might even be comforting Bunny, which would be incredibly awkward.

Once I could muster the energy to get my sweaty body out of the sauna, I'd investigate.

I was hot on the trail.

CHAPTER 26

Everything in the lobby seemed the same. The Cancer Awareness jar was filled to the exact same spot, the lemon infused water jug was still full, and the detectives were still interviewing residents.

One thing different was Ginnie. Was she becoming increasingly more disgruntled? Or maybe I was just more tuned in to her mood? Whichever it was, the change in her disposition was noticeable.

She seemed fidgety, constantly turning in the comfy plush arm chairs. She'd glance off into the distance, even when a detective was talking to her.

It must be difficult to concentrate, if you'd just murdered someone, especially someone like Kip. Then I had an idea. I would start at the Aces' apartment and retrace the Fitbit steps, and I bet it would include a trip to Ginnie's apartment before ending up in the courtyard.

My guess was that Kip went to visit Ginnie before he went to the courtyard. It could have been to see her or tell her he was going to break it off. Then she flipped. Now the pieces were starting to fit together so perfectly.

I put the "Will Be Back Shortly" sign up on the concierge desk. I reset my Fitbit and retraced my steps from Kip's apartment on the 12th floor to Ginnie's apartment—301—and then to the courtyard. It was nearly 623 steps. I knew it. I wish I had been wrong. But Kip must have stopped by Ginnie's apartment early in the morning. It was his pitstop before going to the courtyard. And something told me it wasn't a good visit.

I tried to do as much research as I could from the concierge desk. I checked Kip's Instagram account and was able to find photos of him at golf tournaments, on the golf course, with Bunny at expensive chateaus overseas, and a group photo with his arm around Ginnie. That didn't prove anything though.

I didn't want to believe that Anita was right, but why would she lie about it? What did she have to gain?

Just then, Lillian "cane first" walked up to my desk. "Try and be nice to the residents," she said, faking a smile.

"I'm always nice to the residents," I said.

"Keep them entertained," she said. "We need something they can do, or something to keep them occupied."

"I can ask if they've donated for cancer awareness month," I said, waving the pink-striped glass jar in the air.

"That's not good enough," she said.

"So you think we need a game, or something?" I said, still not following what she was saying. I also still didn't think she had an airtight alibi, so in my eyes I was looking up at a potential killer.

"Think of something," she said. "And maybe I'll accept it as a good resident activity."

With that, she walked away with the loud thud of her cane echoing throughout the lobby.

Just then, Ginnie wandered past the concierge desk. I needed to strike up a conversation with her, but I couldn't think of anything other than the affair and the murder. Yikes!

So I said the first thing that came to mind, "Would you like to donate to cancer awareness month?"

"No, Cassie," she said. "You already asked me that. Like five times. I'd really rather not."

I nodded. "That's fine," I said. "A cup of lemon infused water? We're trying to make this experience as pleasant as possible for all the residents at Parkstone."

"Pleasant? I don't know how this experience could possibly be pleasant," she said.

So that's a no. And people wondered why I felt like I'd never be good at this job.

"A man of greatness has died." Tears welled in her eyes. She got a tissue from her pocket. "And we're all trying to figure out how to go on."

"And who did it," I reminded her. And then I thought I would just go for it. A shot in the dark. "At least, you were able to see him this morning when he was still alive."

"What?" she said, her eyes narrowing.

"When he stopped by your apartment," I said, holding my breath. I had really gone out on a limb here. And my guess was right.

She began stuttering. "H-h-how do you know that?"

"Concierges know more than you think," I said. "A lot more."

Her face blushed and she frowned. "How much do concierges know?"

"He was going to end it, wasn't he?"

She let out a huge sob. Half the lobby turned to look. I waved them away as if there was nothing here to see.

"He ended it," she said, holding a wad of Kleenexes up to her nose. She lowered her voice.

I checked to see if Bunny was in the lobby but she wasn't. The coast was somewhat clear.

She continued, "This morning he told me he wanted to end it with me. All of a sudden, he wanted nothing to do with me. Just in the blink of an eye."

"Why the sudden change of heart?"

"I don't know," she said. "And then he winds up dead!"

"It doesn't look good, that's for sure," I said, trying to remain objective, but knowing that Ginnie had a huge motive. If Eric found out about this, she'd be on his prime suspect list. I'd have to ask Eric if she had an alibi.

"So he just said it's over?" I said.

"You can't say anything to Bunny, all right?" she said. "Just promise me that. It would break her."

Something told me Ginnie should have thought about that before she decided to have an affair with her best friend's husband. But I wasn't going to say anything now. I was only interested if Ginnie was the murderer.

She clutched onto the side of the concierge desk. "Promise?"

"You got it," I said. "I'll do my best, but word around the building is that a lot of people already know. So, good luck keeping it a secret."

She held her hand to her mouth. She sniffled softly. "The consequences of all of this are immense."

"Catastrophic," I said. Then I thought about it some more. "Dare I say, deadly."

And Ginnie let out her loudest sob yet before leaving.

Jet-Setter and Cashmere followed me as they raced over to where Eric sat in the far end of the lobby.

"Does she have an alibi?" I said.

"Who?" said Eric talking in a whisper.

Jet-Setter jumped on top of my lap and purred as Cashmere nestled in on top of the magazines. "Ginnie."

"Yes and no," he said.

"That doesn't sound good," I said.

"She says she was on the phone at the time of the murder. She wasn't on an iPhone. She was using a landline. So we need to get the records from the phone company the old-fashioned way. Could take a while."

"So she has an unconfirmed alibi?" I said, petting Jet-Setter.

"Exactly," he said. "But what she really lacks is motive."

"Not necessarily," I said, giving him a come-hither look. "I've got something you want."

"Tell me about it," he said smiling.

"Meet me in the club room in five," I said, putting Jet-Setter back on the marble floor and heading to the concierge desk to put up the "Will Be Back Shortly" sign.

The club room was the perfect place to talk because nobody was ever in there, even when the Parkstone held events there the turnout was scarce. Everything was in place, as always. When Eric arrived, I gave him a big hug and kiss which I'd been wanting to do all day and night.

"I suspect someone's been missing me," he said.

I smiled. "Guilty as charged."

"So what did you want to tell me about Ginnie?" he said.

"So much," I said, not knowing exactly where to begin. "Basically, she's been having an affair with..." and then I looked around, even though no one was there, and whispered, "Kip."

"No way," he said. "Kip Ace?"

"Yes, Kip Ace," I said. "And apparently Bunny doesn't know about it."

"So, keep it secret," he said. "But also find out if Ginnie killed Kip in a jealous rage?"

"Precisely!" I said, really happy I didn't have to spell it all out for him. "*And*, he broke it off with her yesterday morning."

"There's definitely motive there. I'm going to have to confirm the affair with at least Ginnie," he said. "And really get a solid motive and then wait until I can get her alibi confirmed."

"And I think we may have our murderer," I said.

"It's a process," he said. "We can't assume it's Ginnie, or anyone else for that matter until there's concrete proof."

"What if we don't have time to wait?" I said.

He shook his head. "There's always time. And it's better to get it right."

"Easy for you to say. There's not much time left for me," I said. "I need to clear my name."

"We have at least until the 24 hours are up," he said.

"And if we find the killer before then even better," I said, smiling, confident that Ginnie was it. "Tell me when you have an update on her alibi?"

"You never do give up, do you?"

I smiled, "Would you like me if I did?"

CHAPTER 27

In the club room, I finally thought of something—an activity that everyone at the Parkstone could do: a large 2,000-piece puzzle on the club room shelves that I don't think anyone had ever had the gumption, time, or interest to try.

Now was perfect.

This would keep the residents distracted long enough so that they could enjoy some moments of happiness. This would also give the detectives more one-on-one time with the residents they were interviewing because the lobby would be less crowded.

I pitched the idea to Lillian. "Finally, you thought of something!"

She was relieved, really. I made an announcement on the building overhead system: "Dear Parkstone residents, thank you for bearing with us during this difficult time. In order to show our appreciation, we'd like to invite all of you to the club room for a fun activity and light refreshments."

I also sent out an email invitation just in case residents couldn't hear the overhead. I was hoping for a good turnout.

Five residents showed up: Mr. Gillrot, Mrs. Canterbury, Ginnie Langford, Rich Gibbons, and Anita Halpern, many of whom were on my suspect list.

I dumped the contents of the puzzle box onto the long mahogany table and scattered the pieces. All 2,000 of them. We were going to be here a while.

Mr. Gillrot was first up to the table. "What a wretched idea. I'm just here because it's better than being in the lobby or in my apartment at the moment," he said, eyeing a puzzle piece with disdain.

"We're happy to have you," I said.

"Who's this *we* you talk about?" he said.

"The Parkstone management team."

He grunted. "Some team you got. They let this 24-hour lockdown happen in the first place."

I had to do everything I could to keep from rolling my eyes at him. This had to be about the puzzle, not about Mr. Gillrot's take on the Parkstone's aptitude. "Does anyone else want to help put the puzzle together?"

"Yes, me me me," said Mrs. Canterbury with as much enthusiasm as Mr. Gillrot's disdain.

I handed her a puzzle piece to begin with. She nodded and did a quick curtsy. "Thank you."

Then Rich Gibbons stepped up to the table, "Let's start with the sides. That will be easiest."

"Is easy always the best route?" Ginnie said, examining a puzzle piece. Her emotional terrain seemed grim.

"Can we cut out the philosophical and rhetorical questions, too?" Mr. Gillrot said. "There's just no need for that. Cassie, you're the one who said this should be fun."

I wasn't going to win this. At best we'd have a slight reprieve from the mystery. At worst, we'd have another murder on our hands to solve.

About an hour later, before everyone left the puzzle party, Mrs. Canterbury noticed that there was an oven in the club room. "What's this we have here?" she said.

"Probably the world's oldest oven," I said. The kitchen had been built in the 1960s, with its antiqued cherry cabinets, marble countertops and all stainless-steel appliances that matched with the ornate and vintage décor of the club room.

"Let's bake!" Mrs. Canterbury said. "What better way to pass the time?"

"I'm out," said Mr. Gillrot.

"Somebody might change their mind, when they hear what we're making," Mrs. Canterbury said.

Anita turned her head to the side in thought. "What are we making?"

"Why, let's make something with apples," Mrs. Canterbury said. "I just bought a dozen Granny Smith apples at the store last night before being cooped up in here."

Anita agreed. "That's perfect for the fall. I'm in."

Mrs. Canterbury clapped her hands together, "Then we're all set." She paused. "So, what will it be? How about apple and walnut cake with cream cheese icing?"

"Superb," said Anita. And I agreed it sounded good. What would we do without Mrs. Canterbury?

"I have all the ingredients except the sugar and walnuts. Oh wait, the icing! We'll need cream cheese," Mrs. Canterbury said.

"I have cream cheese," said Rich Gibbons, who was still working on the puzzle. "I prefer it for my bagels, but I guess I could part with some for the cake. How much do you need?"

I thought about Rich's app he was working on with Kip. It sounded like it would be really successful. He seemed reliable and like a team player. A part of me hoped for his sake that he would continue to publish the Ace app.

"One cup would be great," Mrs. Canterbury said. She was glowing.

"How about everyone gets the ingredients," I said. "And we meet back here in ten?"

Mrs. Canterbury had a hand on her forehead. "What else am I forgetting? The sugar!"

"I can bring the sugar," Anita said. "I recently bought a new bag."

"Oh, this is working out perfectly," said Mrs. Canterbury. "Apple cake with cream cheese frosting."

Mr. Gillrot's eyes perked up, his thick eyebrows rising. "I may try some."

"Of course, you will," Mrs. Canterbury said. "It's delicious."

The group departed momentarily to gather the cooking supplies. I pre-heated the oven, and hoped it would work well despite its vintage decorum. I felt the glass oven door. It was beginning to heat up.

There were two large windows in the club room with the curtains open, exposing a view of the courtyard. The curtains were forest green velvet with gold trim and tassels. I couldn't believe what I had discovered just beyond those windows less than 24 hours before. I wanted to close the curtains but then the club room would be dark and lit solely with artificial light.

I was wondering if anyone had been in the club room earlier that morning. If so, they would have seen Kip out in the courtyard. The would have seen who murdered him. If only!

Then Mary Chris Farley's face appeared in my mind. The ghostly look on her face when she was in the lobby after she'd first found out Mr. Ace was murdered. I couldn't get her expression out of my head.

What was it about her? What was it she was hiding? Her face was haunting me.

Those large dark eyes outlined with orange liner. Her long, wavy burgundy hair pulled back at the nape of her neck in a fishtail braid. Her Ralph Lauren outfits were more like uniforms than clothing as she wore them so often. Always ironed, never a wrinkle to be found in a shirt or cord sweater. Nothing ever out of place.

That was enough to drive anyone mad. The image or her ghostly expression was chilling. Something had rocked her world. And I was hoping she'd tell me about it.

Within 30 minutes, the group had returned with mixing bowls, measuring cups and all the ingredients.

"I usually order out," said Anita. "So I may not be the best baker in the group. In fact, I'm pretty sure I'm not."

"I can contribute the cream cheese," Rich said, placing the ingredient on the kitchen island. "And maybe technical assistance if the oven blows a fuse. Other than that, I'll be working on the puzzle."

Mrs. Canterbury threw her hands in the air. "Well, that's fine!" she said. "I love to bake. I can whip this up in no time." She paused. "And I do think Bunny would like a piece."

Mr. Gillrot nodded and crossed his arms. "This batch is for Kip."

The oven beeped which meant it had reached 350 degrees. Mrs. Canterbury scurried to get the ingredients together. Anita helped with the measuring, and I helped with the mixing. Mr. Gillrot read aloud the baking instructions and Rich was absorbed with solving the puzzle.

When the cake was finally in the oven, Mrs. Canterbury said, "Any updates on the mystery?"

I probably wouldn't be able to tell her if there were, but I felt as if Eric had been keeping me out of the loop that I didn't know the latest in the case.

"Not that I know of," I said. "I guess the only update we'll get is when it's solved."

Mrs. Canterbury folded a kitchen towel and hung it over the oven door. "Maybe we're better for it," she said. "If we received constant updates we might all suspect one another."

And then maybe one of us would end up in the oven! I didn't want to think it, but Mr. Gillrot always had such a disdainful look. I stood near the kitchen island. I wasn't going to take my chances.

Then Mr. Gillrot pointed a finger at me. "I'd suspect you, Cassie," he said. "You're the one who found the body."

"That doesn't mean anything," I said, knowing that I was the detectives' prime suspect as well.

"It means opportunity," Mr. Gillrot said. "And opportunity means—"

"End it right there," Anita said. "For all we know, Mr. Gillrot, you were in the courtyard before Cassie discovered the body. That would make you—"

"Stop it!" Mrs. Canterbury said, waving a baking spatula. "Enough murder talk. Let's just enjoy this time that we have to focus on something else."

Everyone smiled at that. I was so grateful for Mrs. Canterbury.

An hour later, the cake was done. The entire club room smelled of delicious baked green apples.

We all crowded around as Mrs. Canterbury sliced the cake. And to my surprise and probably everyone else's, Mr. Gillrot tried a piece. "I hate to say, it's exceptional," he said, "but it is." Then he did something I'd never seen him do before: he smiled.

I didn't think anything could ever put a smile on Mr. Gillrot's face. Leave it up to Mrs. Canterbury!

After we all had generous helpings of the apple cake with cream cheese, Mrs. Canterbury sliced one more piece onto the plate. "Now, who wants to give a slice to Bunny?"

CHAPTER 28

Bunny sat cattycorner to the fireplace in the lobby's far entrance. I wondered if she was cold by the window and if it would be a good idea to light a fire. I'd just need to get some firewood from the parking garage. It would be the least we could do for Bunny.

Her face lit up when she saw me walking over with a plate of apple cake. "You shouldn't have," she said.

"Courtesy of Mrs. Canterbury, Anita Halpern, Rich Gibbons, Mr. Gillrot and myself," I said.

"Mr. Gillrot helped with this?" she exclaimed. "That is quite the group."

"What can I say?" I said sheepishly. "Just trying to pass the time and put a smile on your face."

"Success," she said, taking a bite. "Wow, this is quite good. The walnuts are a nice touch."

"That was Mrs. Canterbury's idea," I said. "She thought it seemed more fall-like with the walnuts."

"Exquisite," she said. Then she seemed to shudder and pulled her shawl up farther around her shoulders. I knew that shawl. It was one I'd picked out for her from Ann Taylor. She needed it for a golf banquet she was going to with Kip.

I looked at the unused fireplace. Why should it go to waste? "I can start a fire," I said. "Normally we don't start using the fireplace until November, but I think we can make an exception."

"A fire would be nice," she said. "Kip always loved fires. We had a fireplace in our apartment on the 12th floor, you know? We used it all the time. Even the smell of burning wood is relaxing."

"Just give me about 15 minutes," I said. "I'll bring up the firewood and you'll be snacking on apple cake in front of a roaring fire in no time!"

I was embracing my own enthusiasm to go above and beyond. Once the Parkstone management saw that enthusiasm I was sure they'd hire me back. Once they saw how happy the residents were, and that I wasn't the killer.

CHAPTER 29

There was only one slight problem: getting the firewood. In order to do so, I'd have to go to the parking garage and load up a dolly with firewood. The only thing is that because of the lockdown, we were not allowed to go into the parking garage. I'd have to ask Eric for permission. I already knew he was going to be less than enthused.

And then it hit me. Kip Ace's car being side-swiped. That mystery hadn't been solved yet either. Who would do such a thing? Maybe it was the same person who murdered him. When I went to the garage for the firewood I could inspect the cars. If that much damage had been done to Kip's car, then the other car involved would be damaged, too.

It was a plan.

I saw Eric writing in his notebook near the courtyard windows.

"Anything new with the case?" I said, knowing the answer was going to be no.

He grimaced. "I wish. We're hitting dead ends everywhere."

"Well, there's something you can do to help."

He must have seen the sparkle in my eye because he said, "If this involves me bending the rules for you, I can't do it."

"You don't even know what I was going to ask," I said.

"Some of the detectives already said I seem distracted," he said. "And I don't want there to be a reputation that I'm not doing a good enough job."

"Well, if you need a tip," I said. "I've got one. Weeks ago, Kip Ace's car was severely side-swiped."

He perked up. "By whom?"

"Nobody knows," I said. "I want to run to the parking garage with a dolly to bring back firewood. That way Bunny will have a fire she'll be happy with. And in the meantime, while I'm getting the firewood, I can check the other cars in the parking lot for damage."

"Well, alright, that's not a horribly inconvenient request," he said, looking unconvinced.

"There's got to be a vehicle that matches the damage on Kip's car," I said. "I just know it."

"Alright," he said. "I'll guard the elevator while you get the firewood and inspect the cars. Be quick though. I'd go with you, but they're going to be suspicious if I'm gone for too long."

"It's okay," I said. "You stand watch."

I managed to steer the dolly to the garage elevators. As Eric stood watch, I took the elevator to the first garage level G1. This is where the firewood was and Kip's car. Two birds with one stone.

I loaded a good amount of firewood onto the dolly. The logs were heavier than I'd thought they would be. Not so much that I couldn't steer the dolly well, but enough that we'd have a fire for the next couple of hours. Now, onto the investigation. I took a look at Kip's car first. The front right passenger side of his Mercedes was severely dented. Much of the black paint had chipped off as well.

Yikes. By the looks of it, somebody really didn't like Kip Ace.

I checked all the cars on the first level and didn't see one with matching damage. I was looking for a car that had damage to the driver's door. I decided to leave the pile of logs and dolly next to the elevator, then go down to G2, the second level parking garage, to see if I could find the car that did this to Kip's Mercedes.

I was checking the cars on G2 as quickly as possible when there it was! A damaged driver's door on a tan Volvo. Some of the black paint from Kip's Mercedes was even streaked on the door. The spot number was number 52. I'd have to remember that.

Whoever owned the car in spot 52 had side swiped Kip's Mercedes and was possibly so angry with him they could have murdered him.

I had the answer. Now I had to get back to the elevators on G1 as quickly as possible. I didn't have much time to spare.

Then I heard rustling. It couldn't be. No one else was allowed to leave Parkstone due to the lockdown.

Then there were more footsteps. They sounded heavy. Somebody else was in the garage. Then the shuffling of feet got closer. A car door slammed shut.

I was so nervous my arms curled like branches. I went to run up the ramp to G1, but froze. The shadow of a large figure towered over me.

"What are *you* doing here?" said the gruff voice.

"What are you?" I said, not yet sure who it was. "Parkstone residents are not supposed to leave the building."

"Technically, this is still part of the building," he said. "The parking garage is part of the building, therefore I haven't left the Parkstone."

I stepped back to get a closer look at the man in shadow. It was Mr. Halpern!

Why was the top advertising executive at GLOW snooping around the parking garage? He gripped his laptop. "Came here to pick up this," he said, waving it in the air. "Can't get much work done without it when Anita's on the computer."

"How'd you get down here?" I said, knowing Eric was covering the parking garage elevators.

"I asked Gilbert, the doorman," he said. "Told him I'd only be a couple of minutes. He said he didn't mind as long as I came back. Even threatened to tell the detectives if I didn't."

"That's good to know," I said.

"What about you?" he said. "Looks like you're up to no good."

"I'm getting firewood for the lobby fireplace," I said.

He looked at me quizzically. "On G2?"

I had to think quickly. "And then I needed to get something from my car," I said.

"But I really should be going back upstairs." I took gaping steps toward the G1 ramp and the elevators.

I'd never been so happy to see firewood in my entire life. Not knowing who else was in the parking garage with me was frightening. Eric would be worried about me. I had to go quickly.

As soon as I got to the lobby, I said hi to Eric who was keeping guard and placed the firewood in front of the fireplace. Back at the concierge desk, I flipped through the assigned parking booklet and gasped!

The resident assigned to spot 52, the mystery suspect, was someone I'd never have guessed in a million years. The spot with the tan Volvo with the dented driver's door belonged to Mrs. Canterbury! Why would she have crashed into Kip's car and then not told him? Was she angry with him? I couldn't see Mrs. Canterbury being upset with anyone for any reason.

The only time I'd seen her even remotely upset was when she'd forgotten chocolate chips at the Safeway.

Mrs. Canterbury couldn't possibly be the murderer. But I needed to know why she'd dented Kip's car.

Eric was sitting in the plush arm chairs in the near end of the lobby. I'd wait to tell him about Mrs. Canterbury being the renter of the parking spot until after I'd spoken with her. I wanted to believe there was some misunderstanding that could easily be understood.

I found Mrs. Canterbury in the club room. There were all the dishes from the apple cake baking piled up in the sink with suds and Mrs. Canterbury was washing them one by one.

"Mrs. Canterbury, you're still here," I said, grabbing a towel to help her dry off the dishes.

"Why yes dear," she said. "I'm so glad the apple cake was a hit."

"I might even try another piece if there's any left," I said.

"You're in luck," she said. "There's one slice left and it has your name on it."

I eyed the slice of apple cake on the mahogany club room table. It looked delicious.

I'd have to ease into asking Mrs. Canterbury about the car. I didn't want to offend her. And I was sure there was a reasonable explanation for it. At least I was hoping so. If not, then I wasn't a good judge of people.

"Mrs. Canterbury," I said, my breath quickening. "Can I ask you a question?"

"Why yes, go ahead, dear," she said, handing me another plate to dry.

"Did you side swipe Kip's Mercedes?"

She gasped and dropped a plate onto the tile. It shattered. This was not what I was expecting. I felt so bad. Mrs. Canterbury was the nicest person I'd ever met.

"How do you know?" she said. Her voice was faint.

I got a broom out from the closet and began sweeping up the glass shards. "I inadvertently discovered it while investigating the crime."

"Well, impressive investigation skills," she said. "A fashionista and a private eye."

I smiled. Mrs. Canterbury always looked on the positive side of life. "I haven't solved the mystery of who killed Kip," I said, "but I happened to notice you did side swipe his car. Were you mad at him for any reason?"

She gasped and put her hand over her chest. "Why no, dear," she said. "Quite the contrary. I get confused. Sometimes in my old age. I accidentally tried parking my car on G1. I drove to where my spot was, and was surprised to see there was a car in the spot next to mine. Kip's car. But I tried to park my car anyway and...good heavens."

"Sounds like an accident to me," I said, knowing that I was barking up the wrong tree. And knowing first-hand there were many more severe car accidents that happened. My thoughts drifted to Hunter. He was so animated and full of life. The hit-and-run just wasn't fair.

"The noise of crushing metal was excruciating," she said, placing her frail hands over her ears.

I bet the sounds of the crash were loud, and that Mrs. Canterbury was shaken. My breath tightened as I heard the noises from Hunter's crash as if it were yesterday. The screeches of the hit-and-run driver pulling away from the scene, and the honks of piled-up cars swerving to the roadside to prevent another death. I shook my head. I couldn't focus. *Concentrate on Mrs. Canterbury*. She looked so shaken. "I'm so sorry to hear that you were confused," I said. "The G1 and G2 levels are not well-lit and when the spot's not well-lit, it can be confusing to know which one is which." My mind was clear of thoughts of the accident. I let out a deep breath. The flashback, for now, was over.

"I was going to tell them the car bump was from me," she said. "But I never had the heart to tell them. Maybe I should tell Bunny?"

I finished dumping the glass shards from the plate into the Hefty trash bag. "That's up to you," I said. "I won't say anything."

She smiled. "Maybe I'll just make Bunny lots of apple cake."

I burst out laughing. "Lucky Bunny," I said. "She did say it was exquisite. And I think someone like Bunny always says what they mean."

"I'll tell her what happened," she said. "Right after the mystery is solved. I don't want to worry her about something like that at a time like this."

"Good call," I said. "And I'll get back to sleuthing to solve this mystery even sooner."

Then she reached for the last piece of apple cake. "Can't do it on an empty stomach."

If there was one person I could count on it was Mrs. "reckless driving" Canterbury.

CHAPTER 30

Other than me versus the murderer, I was staring down another formidable opponent: 15 logs of firewood piled on top of one unwieldy dolly.

Building fires at Parkstone was something I hadn't done since last year. And my manicured hands weren't excited about it. It seemed like it should be man's work. But I couldn't ask one of the male residents to do it, or else I'd probably be fired from my concierge job. Then I remembered I was already fired. So, I contemplated asking the doorman if he could lend a hand and help, but then thought the better of it.

I'd promised Bunny a fire.

I lifted the logs one by one and hoisted them into the fireplace. The excess logs I stacked neatly by the fireplace tools. I crumpled up copies of the days' old newspaper and then lit the fire with kindling.

Only a few chipped nails.

The fire was roaring. "Cassie, this is wonderful," Bunny said. "Better than being alone. You and all the people at Parkstone have been so caring."

What else would we be? I guess there were a few rotten eggs, like Mr. Gillrot, who was a thorn in anyone's side.

Cashmere sat in front of the fire mesmerized by the dancing flames. Her coat was thick, the color of pralines. She pawed at the fluttering flames in front of her. I wondered what I was seeing and missing. What was I pawing at right in front of me that I didn't see?

CHAPTER 31

Back at the concierge desk, there wasn't much new. As if it were a fashion show, residents strutted around the lobby like it was a runway.

Ben Harrison was wearing his green zip-up Under Armour sweatshirt, black jogging pants and sports sandals. Bunny was wearing the shawl I'd picked out for her, culottes, and fluffy slippers with a pom-pom at each end. And then there was Mary Chris Farley's just-in-time-for-Halloween all black ensemble. Dark liner around her eyes gave it added gravitas.

Just like earlier that day, her face looked pale and weathered. Like she'd just been through a storm. I imagined I looked very similar, my hair unkempt, makeup smudged and wearing the same outfit from the day before.

I refused to look in the lobby mirror above the end table because I didn't want to see what I looked like.

Mary Chris looked like death.

She waded through the crowd and slinked up to the concierge desk. Cashmere and Jet-Setter skid onto the desk, landing in front of her.

"Hello, furballs," she said, not cracking a smile. Cashmere pawed at her black sweatshirt. "I'm not really a cat person," she said. "Do you mind?"

"No, of course not," I said, shooing Cashmere and Jet-Setter from the desk. They seemed happy enough to be eating from their food bowls instead.

"What brings you to the desk?" I said, holding up the pink-striped glass jar. "Care to donate for cancer awareness?"

"Look," she said, "I wish it hadn't happened."

I was perplexed. What had happened? I must have looked confused because she said, "That's why you've been giving me weird looks all day. Isn't it?"

"No," I said. Now even more confused than ever. "You look shocked. Like in a state of shock all day. I just noticed. That's all. I haven't been giving you weird looks."

She held her hand to her forehead. "I want to get out of here."

"We all do," I said, resting the pink glass jar back on the desk. I guess now was not the time to be asking residents for donations. "We have to wait until the detectives give us the go ahead."

Then she buried her face in her hands. "I wish I'd never seen him."

"Seen who?" I said, happy she was still talking. A part of me was afraid she would faint.

"Kip!" she said loud enough for other residents to hear. A few of them turned around then went back to their own conversations.

Now I was stunned. "You saw Kip. Yesterday morning?"

She nodded.

"Did you tell the detectives?" I said, hoping Mary Chris wasn't the killer. Hopefully she was just shaken.

"It's on my list of things *not* to do," she said.

"When did you see him?" I said, wanting to know every detail. Mary could be holding a secret clue to the mystery.

"I need to tell someone," she said. "And you're a good listener. You were empathetic when my sink broke the other week. And you were my fashion consultant for the black-tie event I attended last month."

"I promise not to tell," I said, knowing that having a vital clue and not divulging it to Eric was going to be difficult.

She folded her hands together. Her fishtail braid was coming undone with wisps of hair falling around her face. "I saw him yesterday morning when I was walking out through the lobby."

"So you saw him in the lobby?"

"No," she said, looking slightly frustrated with me. "When I was walking through. I saw him on the first floor and we took the stairs together to the lobby level. He continued on to the courtyard—"

"And you walked through the lobby," I said. I wondered what time this was and how it would affect the murder timeframe.

She nodded. "Yes," she said. "And. There's something else."

"What?" I said, gripping the edge of the concierge desk.

"He was crying."

This seemed to fit perfectly with the timeframe of him visiting Ginnie, then he took the stairs to the lobby, and he was probably crying because of the difficult conversation they'd had.

She continued. "Not completely crying, but tearing up. He asked if I was going to the charity golf tournament. When I said yes, he said he had pulled out of the event and that its coordinator was pretty mad at him."

"They were mad at him?" I said. That seemed like a good motive. "Did he say why he pulled out of the tournament?"

"No," she said sharply.

"And then he went out to the courtyard?" I said.

"Yes," she said, nodding slowly.

"You were probably the last person, besides the murderer, to see him alive," I said.

"I wish I wasn't," she said. "It's driving me crazy. I wish I hadn't bumped into him this morning. I'm wondering if it means something."

"I don't think so, but it's interesting to know that the charity event coordinator was upset with him."

Mary threw her hands in the air. "I don't want to know what it means! All I want is to not be the last person to have seen him alive."

"Well you weren't," I said. "The murderer was." The moment I said it, I realized that it wasn't very comforting.

Cashmere purred next to me. At least not everyone was jolted.

"I feel better after telling you," she said. "Cassie, you're a good listener."

I was happy with the compliment. Even Cashmere purred louder.

"Anytime," I said, hitting the concierge bell. Ding!

CHAPTER 32

I logged onto the "Fore the Cure" charity golf tournament website to find out the event charity coordinator who was upset with Kip. It was Luke Beasley! He lived here at the Parkstone. I'd only seen him on a couple of occasions—mainly when he needed something repaired in his 11th floor apartment. I scanned the room and saw him in the far corner of the lobby.

Luke Beasley was balding, shorter than me, which was impressive at my 5'5" stature, and always seemed to be blushing. This is why he never appeared menacing to me at all, in any way. But if what Mary Chris said was true, and I believed her, he had bullied Kip into staying in the charity tournament. Up-to-no-good Beasley.

I saw him in the lobby's far corner, looking at the Parkstone's Halloween decorations, which I'd just put the finishing touches on yesterday. There were haystacks on the floor with pumpkins resting on top. Next to the pumpkins were scarecrows and witches, with pointy hats and long dresses with striped white and black tights.

I liked the striped tights, and thought I wouldn't mind wearing a pair with my Anna Wintour Halloween costume this year. I was happy with how the display had turned out, and judging by the residents' reactions when they'd entered the lobby and were waiting for the elevators, they liked the decor too.

And now, there was the scariest of all: Beasley, who wore a sports jacket with a plaid button-down shirt perfectly tucked into his olive-colored khakis. He wore loafers and styled his hair slicked to one side. He was one of the most well-dressed residents we had. A little *too* well-dressed, even for me.

I decided to go over there and strike up a conversation about the Halloween decorations. "Finding your inner haunt?" I said, thinking maybe he didn't have that far to reach.

"This is real nice," he said. "The witches could look a bit scarier. But all in all, well done."

"Nothing has been scarier around here than the most recent developments," I said.

He looked surprised. "Oh, do they have a suspect?"

I was trying to gauge whether he looked suspicious or worried. He didn't. "No," I said. "But I'm sure they'll find out who did this in no time."

"Good," he said. "Realizing I took strolling outside for granted. And Kip was the finest. He was one of the best golfers out there. Even for his age. Nothing could hold him back." Then he paused. "Didn't listen to anybody. But that's not important."

"Except for maybe you," I said. "He listened to you."

He looked bewildered. "Only when he had to. Surprised I don't have a shiny welt on my forehead," he said. I didn't get it. He continued. "We butted heads a lot."

"Rumor has it he wanted to withdraw from the 'Fore the Cure' charity tournament, and you didn't let him," I said feeling angry on Kip's behalf.

"Now that's not entirely true," he said, a blush spreading across his face. "I told him, correctly, that there was a clause in his contract that required him to give at least two days' notice before withdrawing from the tournament. He just called me about it yesterday morning."

"And you told him he had to compete?" I said.

"I told him the rules," he said. "After all, I am the chairman. And if players want to play in the charity tournament, there are rules to play by."

"And you couldn't make just one exception," I said. "Even for the finest?"

"Look," he said. "You get it. I know you do. Kip had thousands of fans. He brought in a lot of money to the tournament. If Kip didn't play, we'd lose the fan base, the concession sales, the viewership. All in the pond. All in the pond because Kip decided to bail."

"Maybe he wanted to spend more time with his family?"

Luke waved his hands in the air. "I don't know the reason. All I know is he signed a contract and he had sworn to play today." Then he paused. "Except, well, he did find a way out of it."

I gasped. "Kip was murdered. That's no laughing matter."

"And when I told him there was no way out of the deal, I hadn't really thought of *that*."

"Well, no one had," I said, nervously playing with my fountain pen necklace. I didn't think Luke was our suspect. But I did think he was a money-digging scoundrel. But he didn't have enough anger in him. Especially not toward the revered Kip.

"I've already talked with the detectives," he said. "You can't blame any of this on me. Although I'd like to see them try. I was making calls all morning to prepare for the charity event. They checked my iPhone's call log and everything checks out. Had actually put a call in to Kip right about the time they say he was murdered."

I gasped and nervously dropped my fountain pen necklace. It took me a second to regain my composure. I'm sure Kip was happy to miss Luke's call. All Luke saw in Kip was dollar signs.

I rearranged the cloth witches sitting atop the haystack. I thought about what Luke had said about Kip wanting to withdraw from the tournament. And possible motives. Something was awry.

Just then Mr. Graham approached the concierge desk. He had already donated to the cause and I didn't want to bother him about that again. Cashmere and Jet-Setter raced to the countertop, with Cashmere almost sliding off with all the momentum.

"Wait up, Cashmere," I said, pulling her back so she wouldn't fall off the desk.

"Do you have time to talk?" Mr. Graham said. I'd never before seen him this serious.

"Well, I'm not going anywhere until this case is solved," I said. "So the answer is yes."

He looked relieved. "The story's getting out of control."

"What story?" I said.

"The story of the murder here. Kip's murder. They are saying there's a poison murderer at the Parkstone. And that they're going to strike again."

"Who's saying this?" I said.

"The news. Channel 5," he said. "I still have some friends at the station and they're all asking me to comment. They want me to confirm whether that story is true."

"It's not true," I said. "So untrue. Kip was killed with a blunt object."

"They have an anonymous source who says he was poisoned," he said.

I shuddered. I held tight to Cashmere. "Well, we have to make sure they get the story right. We have to make sure they know that's not true."

"I tried," he said. "The problem is that if they have an anonymous source, they can go ahead with the story."

Cashmere squirmed out of my grip. This was horrible. I covered my face with my hands. Someone was leaking false information to the press. Could it be the killer, covering their tracks by throwing off the media?

"All of this is out of my control," Mr. Graham said. He petted Jet-Setter. "I don't even work at the station anymore." Then he looked up. "Thank God."

"Well, we've got to think of something," I said. "We can't let misinformation get out there about the crime."

I was incredulous. I couldn't believe what Mr. Graham was telling me. "Who would make up such lies?" I said.

"And you haven't heard the worst of it," he said.

Dear God, there was more? "I don't think it can get much worse," I said.

"It can," he said. "And it did."

I braced myself for the worst. He continued. "They're saying it's you!" My heart sank. I knew that's what the detectives were thinking, but now it was going to be telecast. What would residents think of me? Some, like Mr. Gillrot, already scorned me. But others really thought I was great.

Now someone was trying to turn the tide by putting all the blame on me. Who would do that? There's only one person I could think of and that would be the killer.

"I'll do what I can," he said. "If you think of a way to stop it, let me know." He paused. "Or if you find out who's divulging the info I'd love to know."

That made two of us. "And if you find out any more info, you know where to find me," I said, placing the "Will Be Back Shortly," sign on the desktop. I'd be back. Just right after I talked to Eric, who was talking with Rich Gibbons. When he caught my eye, he must have sensed it was something urgent because he stopped the conversation immediately and walked right over.

He put a strong hand against the wall, leaning in so close I could smell his cologne. "What's wrong?" he said, wiping a tear that had welled up in my eye.

"Everything," I said, doing my best to keep myself together.

"Is something wrong between us?" he said.

"No," I said, fighting back another tear.

"See, so not everything is bad."

Eric was always smarter than me. I usually liked that about him. Right now, it wasn't so endearing. "All of the detectives think I'm the prime suspect, and now so does the media."

"The media?" he said. "I can assure you none of the detectives gave them that impression."

"They didn't have to," I said looking down at my feet, at my fluffy slippers. "A resident took it upon themselves to leak false information to the press."

"Oh Geez, Cassie, I'm sorry," he said. He held my hand tightly in his. Our fingers fit together perfectly. They always had. Ever since he had first held my hand when we were twenty years old. "Look, I can't change that. If they ask me for a soundbite, I'll give them one: There's been a murder at Parkstone, and the killer is still on the loose. The building is on a 24-hour lockdown as detectives conduct interrogations and search for clues."

"And that's all there is to know about the Parkstone case." That made me even sadder.

He took my hand, spreading my fingers apart then clasping them together again. "Exactly," he said. "I wish we had more information at this time, but the truth is, we don't."

"I'm about to get dragged though the mud on television," I said. "What are our chances of having a dinner date tomorrow night?"

"It all depends if we catch the killer," he said.

"Which means *you* should probably get back to work."

"I'm detecting hostility," he said with a smile.

"I'm the prime suspect in a murder case, and I'm innocent," I said.

"And the hostility isn't helping."

I nodded. "Got it. I guess that would be the main trait of a murderer."

He flipped his notebook open. "Yep. Should I be taking notes?"

CHAPTER 33

I had to tell someone the bad news. Eric was a conflict of interest in all of this. He was my boyfriend of fifteen years, but he was also the lead homicide detective on the case. He liked chasing down the bad guy more than he liked me. Or so it seemed. And even though he was trying to help me clear my name, he also had his job to do as a detective.

I grabbed my cellphone from behind the concierge desk and walked to the club room. I knew it was early in the morning, but I also knew that my mom always loved hearing from me. So I called my mom at 6:30 in the morning, which was 4:30 a.m. all the way in Cherry Creek, Colorado. I wondered if the Parkstone murder mystery had made national headlines, or was her only knowledge of the murder based on the frantic text messages I had sent her yesterday?

Even though my phone call had awakened her, my mom was positive about the murder mystery situation, most likely to keep my spirits up. "Everything will work itself out," she said. "It's got to."

She was right. The mystery had to resolve itself at some point. How it would resolve itself was the question. "But what if it doesn't?" I said, always the pessimist to my mom's optimism. "Royce Baxter already doesn't want me manning the concierge desk, which means I need to find another job in Bethesda after this is over because there's no way I'm moving back to Cherry Creek."

I had a feeling that might be disappointing to her, but Eric lived on the East Coast now, and I didn't plan on leaving him any time soon.

"Sweetie, your boss may change his mind about that," she said. "If you weren't on time to make the building rounds like you were supposed to, then he has grounds to be upset. That doesn't mean he won't re-think your value as a concierge and possibly change his opinion."

Something told me when Royce Baxter made his mind up about something there was no turning back.

My mom continued, "You're on the front lines there. You can sit around and feel sorry for yourself or you can make something happen. Why don't you team up with Eric and see what happens?" She paused. "By the way, how are you two?"

My mom was probably sitting in the kitchen that smelled of home-baked pumpkin bread and getting ready to watch the sunrise through the vast kitchen windows. She was probably looking out onto the deck where she hosted summer soirees, and where we'd share iced tea or hot chocolate depending on the season. Her backyard was glorious. There was even a hummingbird who would fly up to the feeder near the kitchen window. Why didn't I want that enviable low-key life?

It wasn't that I was unhappy there. It's just that I'd much rather be in a larger, upscale city with more excitement and more fashion. And I knew a lot of it had to do with Hunter, too.

"Eric and I are good," I said. "He's really busy working on the case right now, so I see him here and there, but we haven't had much time to talk." I tried to look on the bright side. "At least we're in the same place."

"I'm glad you two have each other," my mom said. Then sounding a bit sad she said, "And has he proposed yet?"

This was a sore spot. "You'd be the first to know if he had." It made me wonder why she asked.

"What I don't understand is that you moved all the way out to the East Coast for him, and after 15 years still no real commitment?" she said. "At what point do you cut your losses?"

I was silent. I had to try my best to keep from crying. It seemed like everything was a mess at that moment— the murder, my keeping a job, mine and Eric's relationship. And the fact that I hadn't just moved out here for Eric. Then she continued, "Dear, I fear that you have lost your way. I think a lot of it has to do with your coping with Hunter's death."

I still wasn't over his death and didn't know when I would be, because I still wondered what life would be like if the hit-and-run hadn't happened. The day was still burnished in my mind. The day he and I were walking across the crosswalk on Hyacinth Blvd. The first lane of cars stopped for us, but the driver in the second lane of cars didn't see Hunter as he walked out and was hit by the vehicle. I was so focused on Hunter that I didn't get the license plate number or car make, which to this day still weighs heavy on my heart.

Finding Kip's dead body in the grass had brought back all of those old memories that were part of the reason I'd left Cherry Creek.

I gulped down tears. "Maybe," I said, holding the phone closer to my ear. Colorado was sounding far away. "I still can't believe they never caught the hit and run driver."

"I think that case is closed, but I understand that it's difficult to come to terms with. I know you have Eric out there in Bethesda," she said, "but you picked up and left in such a hurry and I'm not sure it was for the best. You're working in a fancy part of town, hobnobbing with people much richer than how you were raised. And I feel like you're losing yourself in them. You're losing your way. You are so attentive to them and wrapped up in their lives, that I fear you aren't paying attention to your own."

"I'm still the same person," I said.

"Apparently you're not," she said. "Now you're the prime suspect in a murder case."

I breathed in a deep breath. She had a point. The truth was when I was wrapped up in other people's lives, I could forget about my own. I didn't even have real friends. The only people I talked to were my mom and Eric and the residents. "I'm mostly the same person."

"That's true, but your own boyfriend, who can figure out murder plots, can't figure out how to commit to you after 15 long years." She took a deep breath. There was a long pause. "And you're waiting. I just don't want to see you lose yourself because you're running away from something."

Now the tears that had welled up in my eyes were streaming down my face. Maybe I *had* lost my way. But if I had, I wasn't sure I wanted it back. I couldn't live my life in the same town thinking about what had happened to Hunter. Everything in Cherry Creek reminded me of him: our walks and talks along the creek, the movie theater where we'd sneak in and watch two movies in a row, and his father's cigars he used to smoke.

I liked working at the Parkstone and helping residents. It helped me forget everything else. There were just a couple things out of place in my life that I needed to adjust.

"I can't help it, Mom," I said. "I'm wrapped up in the residents' lives, and I'm becoming obsessed with this case for better or worse."

"This case is tangled up now, but eventually it's going to unfold," she said, "and something tells me you'll be at the heart of it when it does."

"I hope that's a good thing," I said.

"And I know Royce Baxter is upset you weren't on time for rounds, but between us, I'm happy you weren't there when you were supposed to be. You could have been in harm's way. Who knows what could have happened if you were in the courtyard with Kip and the murderer? I think the fact that you were late worked out for the best."

I said goodbye to my mom. And wiped tears from my eyes.

Before returning to the concierge desk, I flipped on the TV in the club room. There was the Channel 5 News morning reporter standing in front of the Parkstone's building entranceway and the words *Breaking News* scrolled along the bottom of the screen.

"This just in," the reporter said, placing a finger on the earphone in his ear. "New details in the murder and theft here at the exclusive Parkstone."

Theft? That means a resident had spilled the beans about the box of t-shirts that were stolen from my apartment.

"Resident and Parkstone concierge, Cassandra Hall, is said to be the prime suspect in the poisoning of pro-golfer and millionaire Kip Ace..."

Poisoning? I clicked off the TV. Someone was leaking false information to the media. This wasn't fair. I couldn't take it anymore. The mystery was unfolding alright, and I was at the center of it. I was going to solve this case if I had to upturn every nook and cranny at Parkstone!

CHAPTER 34

If I wanted to solve this crime I had to act now. I sat next to Bunny on the plush arm chairs and offered to bring her a warm beverage.

"No, thank you," she said. "I'm quite all right. Probably going up to my room here in a bit."

"I understand," I said. "I'm sure you just want to get away from everything."

"Yes, that's exactly what it's like," she said.

I knew the feeling. "Well, I won't take up too much of your time," I said. "It's just that, I urge you, if you can remember anything, anything about the morning, let me or the detectives know."

"I really can't," she said. "I was up in our apartment getting ready for brunch. I was going to wear a lovely peach peplum blouse with skirt and gloves."

"That outfit sounds dashing," I said. "I'm sure you would have looked gorgeous."

"Nothing out of the ordinary this morning that I can remember," she said, "but there is something." She lowered her voice. "And I didn't tell the detectives, because I'm not sure I want to make a big deal about it. He really is a well-intentioned man."

"Who?" I said.

"Mr. Gillrot," she said.

Well-intentioned, or well, just plain irritating. Mr. Gillrot was by no means a well-intentioned man. But I wasn't going to argue with the widow.

She continued, "Well, about a couple months ago, Mr. Gillrot had trouble paying rent. He came to Kip with an idea: Kip would purchase a one-of-a-kind bottle of 1947 Chateau Cheval Blanc that had been in Mr. Gillrot's family for years. And Mr. Gillrot would have enough to pay his rent for quite some time." She paused for a moment. "This is why we had the wine photographer coming yesterday. Kip had wanted the entire collection photographed now that it was complete."

"Seems like it was a win-win," I said.

"Not quite. Mr. Gillrot—once he got financially stable again—wanted the bottle back," she said. "Imagine that! He wanted to buy back the bottle Kip had already purchased. Kip didn't want to sell it."

"I can see where that would get dicey," I said.

"Well, Kip didn't give in," she said. "He kept the bottle for his collection and Mr. Gillrot was mad with envy. And that was that."

"Until that wasn't enough," I said, thinking that Mr. Gillrot then decided to get even and get that bottle back for good. "And it's a 1947 Chateau Cheval Blanc?"

"Very difficult to find."

Mr. Gillrot had killed Kip Ace, I was sure of it! Maybe he'd gotten wind of the photo shoot and that's why he'd let his anger loose today. So he threw a golf club over his balcony and bolted Mr. Ace right in the head!

He wasn't going to get away with this. I said goodbye to Bunny and thanked her for the nugget of information—what a gem! A part of me was thinking I should mention it to Eric first. But since Bunny didn't want to tell the detectives, it wasn't really my place to, right?

But first, I needed to see if the golf club that had been found with Kip was one that belonged to Mr. Gillrot. I thought back to the morning. The golf club at the scene had a light blue tape on the grip.

I checked my pocket to make sure I had my keys and I made my way to the elevator.

"Where are you going?" Eric slid in front of me before I could step onto the elevator.

"Up to my apartment to grab something," I said.

"All right," he said. "Don't go too far for too long though, okay? Things are heating up with this case. And I worry about you."

I was listening to Eric, but I was also looking around to make sure that Mr. Gillrot was in the lobby and there'd be no running into him in his apartment. Check.

"I'm fine," I said.

"Alrighty," he said, moving from in front of the elevator. "I believe you."

A part of me wished I could tell Eric about my new lead on the case. But in a way, that seemed like more of a risk. And it would slow things down considerably.

I took the elevator to the 12th floor and went to Mr. Gillrot's apartment. I turned the key and I was in! I quietly locked the door behind me and searched for his golf clubs. They weren't in the hallway, the living room or the kitchen. Nor the bedroom. Maybe the closet. I turned the handle and found the golf clubs there. They all had a light blue grip. This was the same set as the golf club that had been found at the crime scene.

That's them! I knew that was them. It was Mr. Gillrot's golf club that had killed Mr. Ace, and I bet he was the one who'd thrown it. Who else would have had access to Mr. Gillrot's golf clubs?

My heart was beating so fast that small fluttering beats felt like one large thump. I closed the closet door only to hear someone's footsteps coming down the hall. And whistling. It was Mr. Gillrot!

I made sure everything was how I found it. And jumped back into the closet next to the golf clubs. I was surrounded by Mr. Gillrot's coats and it smelled slightly of mothballs.

The floorboards creaked as Mr. Gillrot walked down his hallway past the closet. Then his footsteps stopped. Did he notice something out of place? Did he know I had broken into his apartment? My nerves were so rattled I thought I was going to scream. I grabbed my stomach to stop from yelling.

Creak. Then the footsteps continued again to the bathroom. The door shut.

Now was my chance.

I quickly opened the closet door and stepped out from among the long jackets. I closed the door behind me and creeped out to the foyer and eventually out the door, just as I heard the toilet flush.

Phew. I took a deep breath. I could breathe again.

I ran to the staircase at the end of the hallway. I decided to go to the penthouse floor next. I wanted to go to the wine cellar and see the bottle Bunny had been talking about. Then I remembered I'd told Eric I'd be back shortly. I didn't want him to worry and come looking for me.

So I headed back to the lobby where Mrs. Canterbury greeted me with a warm hello. "I made apple cider, my dear," she said. "Would you like to try some?"

How could I say no to either Mrs. Canterbury or apple cider?

"Yes, of course," I said. "That sounds great."

"One full mug just for you," she said, handing me a floral printed mug filled to the brim.

"People are getting antsy, aren't they?" she said, looking around the lobby.

"It's bothering a lot of people," I said. "I know that. I think everyone is just doing the best they can." *Everyone except for Mr. Gillrot*, I thought whose golf clubs were the murder weapon, I was certain. He had a motive, too. According to Bunny, he was upset about selling his family's prized wine possession. That's a motive if I've ever heard one.

"Anything new with the case?" Mrs. Canterbury said. "I asked the detectives, but they're pretty secretive, aren't they?"

"Yes," I said. "I haven't heard an update from them recently."

"I thought maybe I could woo them with apple cider," she said. "But that didn't work."

I smiled. Mrs. Canterbury was always so pleasant. "I'll let you know when and if I hear anything. And thank you for the apple cider. It's really delicious."

"Anytime, dear," she said, patting me on the shoulder. "And do keep me in the loop."

Jet-Setter ran circles around my legs and then followed Mrs. Canterbury as she walked to the far end of the lobby.

I finished the apple cider and placed the mug on top of the concierge desk. I made sure I had the keys and headed for the elevator. Time to check out the wine cellar.

Taking the elevator to the top penthouse floor seemed to take forever. Ping!

The penthouse floor seemed quieter than usual. Maybe that's just because I felt like I was sneaking around. And I probably felt that way because I *was* sneaking around the entire building.

I unlocked the temperature-controlled wine cellar room and walked all the way to the far end where Mr. Gillrot's wine cellar room was located. I quickly turned the switch to find hundreds of wine bottles and Mr. Gillrot standing in the middle of the room holding the bottle of 1947 Chateau Cheval Blanc!

I gasped! It was too late to turn around now. "Mr. Gillrot," I said, my voice shaking. "What are you doing here?"

"This is my wine cellar," he said. "I pay extra in rent for it. What about you? Snooping around? Thinking you're solving the crime."

"I'm smarter than you think," I said. "I know that your golf club was found at the scene of the crime. You killed Mr. Ace!"

"I did no such thing," he said, clutching the 1947 Chateau Cheval Blanc bottle. "I threw that golf club into the courtyard toward Mr. Ace after I'd heard him yelling back and forth with some woman."

"You threw it into the courtyard and it whacked Mr. Ace in the head, killing him," I said.

"No such thing happened," he said. "Where did you get that into your head?"

"That's exactly what happened," I said. "How else could he have died except with your golf club? And you just admitted to throwing it."

He began to move toward the door with the bottle. I stepped in front of him and grabbed onto one end of the bottle.

"Let go!" he snarled. I tugged harder. He scrunched his nose so hard his dagger-shaped teeth showed. "I said let goooooooo!"

I also had a hunch Mr. Gillrot had stolen the t-shirts. He was always hanging around the concierge desk so he knew where the key ring was, and he clearly didn't want me investigating the case. "*And* you stole the t-shirts!" I said, figuring now was as good a time as any to confront him.

He clutched the bottle to his chest. "A couple of lousy t-shirts," he said. "I wanted you to get your nose out of this case."

So he did steal them!

"How dare you!" I said, tugging the bottle toward me fiercely. "Those were t-shirts I designed for a charity event."

"Now you know how it feels to have something you care about taken from you," Mr. Gillrot said, staring at the wine bottle.

"The bottle *wasn't* taken from you," I said. "You sold it!"

I tugged harder. Mr. Gillrot lost his grip on the neck and the bottle crashed to the floor. Broken pieces stuck up around our shoes as the wine seeped into a puddle around us. Mr. Gillrot's entire face turned downward.

"Why you little twerp!" he said, glaring at me. He hovered over me for a second then pushed me toward the farthest rack and shut the door.

I was in the temperature-controlled wine cellar all by myself, and the temperature controls were on the outside. The cellar became cooler and cooler. I'm the type of person who feels cold when it's hot outside and there's a breeze. This was becoming unbearable.

The temperature was plummeting. And fast!

CHAPTER 35

The hairs on my arms began to rise as the chill set in to my bone. I'd have to find a way out, but how? There were no windows—it was like a giant ice box. The lock locked from the outside.

What I'd give for some of Mrs. Canterbury's hot apple cider now, I thought. Or maybe a cashmere shawl. I remembered spending time in the wine cellars on tours with new residents. It was offered as an amenity. Now it was a death trap.

I had to focus.

I remembered one time I'd gotten locked in my walk-in closet and didn't have my cellphone on me like now. And I was able to take apart the pen in my necklace and pick the lock.

I removed my necklace and walked around the broken glass shards toward the door. The cold was getting even colder and was slowing my movements. I rapidly rubbed my hands along my arms to warm them up, which offered me seconds of warmth here and there.

My hands were so cold they trembled as I took apart my necklace. I took the pen piece out and attempted to pick the lock. My hands were trembling so much I dropped the thin pen.

I breathed on my hands. That warmed them up enough for me to be able to grab the pen. I was without help. No one would find me here. I should have listened to Eric and stopped investigating. Confronting a killer was beyond me.

I breathed on my hands again. *Here goes nothing*!

This time I was able to place the pen in the lock. I moved it up, and bingo! The door opened. Phew! I fell out through the door and onto the ground. I was so relieved to be out of the wine cellar that I sat there on the floor, shivering for a couple of moments before moving.

There wasn't too much time to spare. I'd have to go back to the lobby and tell Eric that Mr. Gillrot was the killer. He had motive and the murder weapon. Sealed case.

I got up and walked down the penthouse hallway when I saw Mr. Gillrot walking towards me from the other end. "Why you little rat!" he said. "You owe me thousands of dollars for that bottle."

I couldn't afford another confrontation with him. And that bottle wasn't even his. It had belonged to Kip. The next trap with him I might not be able to get out of. I was close to a small door on my right that led to a dumbwaiter.

"You're going to pay for what you did," I said.

"For the last time," he said, "I didn't kill Mr. Ace. Didn't like him. But didn't kill him."

If I could fit in the door, I'd be able to take the dumbwaiter to the club room on the first floor and then find Eric and tell him Mr. Gillrot was the murderer.

I eyed the size of the door. I thought I could fit. And I was right. Now I just hoped it could hold my weight—all 120 pounds of me—until I made it safely to the club room. I scrunched my knees to my chest and held onto the rope for the dumbwaiter, making sure I was going down the tunnel in a slow, consistent way.

Mr. Gillrot was still yelling at me from the top. "Well, that oughta teach ya!" he said.

I moved my hands faster and faster down the rope, and his voice—echoing within the walls of the dumbwaiter—receded. More than anything, I wanted to get away from him. I needed to find Eric. Why hadn't I listened to Eric when he had been worried about my sleuthing? There were cobwebs that I wanted to sway at, but I couldn't take my hands off the rope. My breathing quickened and I sensed I was approaching the first floor. *How many more floors until the club room?* My arms moved faster and faster, then I saw the approaching cement floor, and I knew I was almost there. When I reached the club room door, I breathed in deeply.

I was almost there, and I was hoping Mr. Gillrot wasn't on the other side waiting for me. Careful to steady myself, I pushed open the door with my comfy slippers. As it flung open, I crawled out onto the club room counter where I had just made a cake with Mrs. Canterbury hours before.

I'd made it! I jumped off the counter and surveyed the room. Mr. Gillrot wasn't in sight and I couldn't have been happier to be on the 1st floor of the Parkstone.

I looked toward the mahogany table, and there was Rich Gibbons holding a puzzle piece. "Rich?" I said.

"Cassie?" he said, looking confused, "where does that lead?"

"It's the dumb waiter," I said.

"What were you doing in there?"

I wanted to say I was escaping the crazy resident Mr. Gillrot, but didn't want to call attention to the entire, he-tried-to-freeze-me-in-the-wine-cellar-and-might-be-a-murderer thing. "The elevator was taking forever," I said. "I thought it would be a shortcut."

"That's really cool," he said. "I wish I could find a shortcut for this puzzle. I'm a computer programmer and this is taking me a long time to solve."

"I'm glad you're keeping at it," I said. At least someone liked my puzzle idea.

The clubroom looked glorious. It smelled like new. It always did. The curtains were ajar and the light soaked in. I tried to bask in the warmth.

I checked the hairs on my arms to make sure they hadn't frozen off. I needed to find Eric. I said goodbye to Rich and wished him luck with the puzzle. I headed back to the lobby where people were milling around.

It was more crowded than usual. Bunny looked like she was weeping in one of the plush chairs near the Chihuly sculpture. What a sight. She looked so lonely. So alone.

She would get through this. And I thought it would help her to find the killer. I saw Eric in the far corner of the lobby sipping a cup of coffee and talking with another detective.

I hated to interrupt, but this was important. "Detective," I said, "I have something important to tell you."

"Where have you been?" he said, looking relieved to see me. "I was about to go looking for you."

"I'm fine," I said, "and I know who the killer is."

"You know who you *think* it is," he said.

"It's Mr. Gillrot," I said. "He has a motive, and the golf club used as a murder weapon is his."

"Mr. Gillrot?" he said. "But that can't be."

"Oh, yes it can," I said. "And he just tried to lock me in a wine cellar on the penthouse floor."

I must have been talking really fast because Eric asked me to slow down. "What? Locked you in the penthouse wine cellar? Why? It's not him," he said. "He has an airtight alibi."

"He does?" I said, completely shocked.

"Yes, he was in the gym at the time of Kip's murder," he said. "He's not the murderer. He's not a suspect we're considering." Then he looked at me more sternly. "And you're not considering him as a suspect either, right?"

"Right," I said, still not believing Mr. Gillrot's alibi. "How do you know he's telling the truth?"

"There's video footage on the surveillance camera that shows him in the gym," Eric said.

"At the time of the murder?" I said.

"At the time of the murder," he said. "Case closed."

"Case closed," I said, crossing my frozen-to-the-bone arms in defeat. "But he did lock me in a wine cellar," I said.

"Are you okay?" he said. "There are serious ramifications if he did that."

Just then there was banging on the front door. It was a FedEx delivery. There was loud knocking again. The FedEx delivery driver was very impatient. I'd have to continue my conversation with Eric later.

I moved quickly to the door and opened the heavy lobby doors. "Welcome to Parkstone," I said.

"Yeah, yeah, yeah," he grumbled. He was holding a large crystal vase of red roses.

"Beautiful," I said.

He rolled his eyes. "Sign here," he said, holding out the signature pad.

I wondered who was the lucky recipient. I always wondered that when a resident got a nice package or flowers. Maybe it was someone who knew a resident was on lockdown and wanted to brighten their day? That would be thoughtful.

The FedEx delivery driver grunted goodbye. And as I closed the Parkstone lobby doors, I took a quick peek at the letter nestled in the roses: "Bunny, I'm so sorry. Yours always, Kip."

I gasped! The roses were for Mrs. Ace, and they were from Kip. He must have sent them before he was murdered. What was he sorry for? I brought the roses to the concierge desk and looked around for Mrs. Ace but she wasn't in the lobby.

It must be the affair.

Could he be apologizing for cheating on her with Ginnie? Which would mean she knew about the affair with her best friend! She knew about the affair—the words were sinking in. And that dark feeling I had earlier turned ten times darker. She must have been really upset: motive. And she must have found out recently because the flowers just arrived today. That fits within the time frame of rage.

And what was her alibi? I didn't want to make the same mistake twice and think it was a suspect who had an airtight alibi. I remembered she mentioned something to me about getting ready for brunch. She said she was going to get ready for brunch and wear a peplum blouse, skirt and gloves. I never forget an outfit.

And that's not what she was wearing when she first walked off the elevator and the detectives told her the bad news. So what prevented her from getting ready and wearing the cute brunch outfit? Murder? After Mr. Gillrot threw the golf club down to the courtyard, Mrs. Ace could have run down there, picked it up, and upset with Mr. Ace about the affair, clocked him over the head with the nine iron.

I tracked down Eric. "Quick question," I said. "And I need an answer, fast."

"Shoot," he said.

"Mrs. Ace," I said. "What's her alibi?"

"She was doing laundry at the time of the murder," he said.

My heart sank. "That's impossible," I said. The maintenance team was working on the pipes from 7-10 this morning. There was no way Bunny would have had water to do laundry. "The water system was shut off this morning during the hours Bunny claimed she was doing laundry."

Eric whipped out his notebook to scribble down what I was saying. "So Bunny, his wife, doesn't have an airtight alibi."

Forget the notebook, I thought, *we don't have a lot of time.* I looked around the lobby. "Where's Bunny now?"

His face looked so sullen. I didn't give up. "Where is she?" I said. "I'll check her apartment."

"No need to," Eric said. "I told her she could grab something from her car."

"The parking garage!" I said. We needed to catch her. "We've got to go. We're off to G1." Jet-Setter in tow!

"Wait, it's a process. First I need to log a report that her alibi was false."

"We don't have time for process," I said. "The 24-hour lockdown is almost lifted, we haven't slept all night, and we have a killer who has the means to leave the country if we don't get to her first."

Eric grimaced.

"I don't have time to wait," I said, running toward the elevator. Ping! It was already here. Jet-Setter scurried in behind me. "Are you in?"

"I'm trusting you," he said, stepping onto the elevator. I pressed the G1 level.

"I no longer want to be the main suspect," I said. "And solving this case is the only way to do it."

In the parking garage, Bunny was stuffing her packed Louis Vuitton suitcase into the trunk of her Mercedes.

"Not so fast," I said.

"Hands up," Eric said. When she didn't respond, he shouted, "Now!"

Bunny gave up on her suitcase and hoisted her hands in the air in a dramatic fashion. "I'm innocent," she said. "I was doing laundry."

"That's impossible," I said. "The water was shut off from 7-10 this morning by maintenance."

She blushed. "Well, I don't know the exact time I was doing laundry," she said.

"You were also picking out an outfit to wear to brunch," I said. "At least that's the alibi you told me."

"Yes, that's what I was doing."

Both Eric and I shook our heads. Even Jet-Setter scowled.

"So which one is it?" Eric said.

"There was so much confusion this morning," she said. "It's amazing I was thinking straight at all."

I gave her a look of being unconvinced. She burst out into angry sobs again. Then before we knew it, she jumped in the car and ploughed it into reverse.

"She's making a run for it," I said.

She sped past Eric. As the car nearly sideswiped him I had a flashback to Hunter walking in front of me before being hit by the car. It had all happened so suddenly. Eric fell to the ground from the car's force. Then he was moving. He was okay. But, I felt hopeless again. I had to close my eyes tightly to stop the flashback. We couldn't lose Bunny. I lunged forward to the wall with the red button that controlled the parking garage gate. She sped up. She was going to escape. I pressed the button as quickly as possible.

The gate descended. Bunny accelerated the Mercedes, but not quick enough. The garage gate trapped the hood of her car.

"Hands up," Eric said, "and out of the car. Keep 'em where I can see 'em."

I hung back behind one of the garage banisters. When I saw Bunny had stepped out of her car and had her hands on the roof, I emerged. Her voice was shaky.

"It's just that you don't know what it's like to have a husband who doesn't give you the time of day. If it's not one thing, it's the other. Today it was the charity event, that's why he couldn't spend time with me. The charity event! And then he decides to cheat on me with my best friend. Do you know how humiliating that is?"

"He sent you a dozen red roses," I said. "With a note saying he was sorry. They're sitting on the concierge desk now as we speak. Thought you should know."

"Oh, Kip," she said. "I really didn't mean to. It was always just too little too late."

"Well, now you don't have to worry about it. Now all you have to worry about is jail time," I said, as Eric placed handcuffs on her. I thought about yesterday morning and hearing a faint scream and seeing, what I didn't know at the time was Bunny, the dark shadow flickering along the row of trees.

Eric turned to me. "Nice work," he said. "I'm going to be taking her to the station. And tonight I'm taking you out to dinner. Rest up."

CHAPTER 36

Eric and the other detectives took Bunny away in the police car to the station. I was so relieved the murder was solved and my life could go back to revolving around suntans, stylish outfits and dinner dates with Eric.

And, of course, the residents. My life wouldn't be full without hearing their stories and sharing their joy. I was just so relieved. The 24-hour ban was lifted and residents could come and go as they pleased.

Mrs. Canterbury sauntered up to the concierge desk. "You know, dear, I got to thinking," she said. "We should do something for Kip."

"It really is tragic, isn't it?" I said, thinking of how much Bunny's life was going to change too.

"Tragic, yes," she said. "We see this all the time at the NIH. Not murders, but people's lives changing, and here we are in the throes of it. Patients receive good news or bad news about a certain disease or drug. And we're with them every step of the way."

"Do you have any more of that apple cider?" I said.

"Why, of course I do!" she said. "Get out your mug."

I got out the floral mug she'd given my earlier. She poured the apple cider to the brim. It was so warm and comforting.

"So what do you suggest?" I said.

"How about renaming the courtyard?" she said.

I smiled. "To Kip's Crabapple Tree Courtyard?"

"That sounds good to me," she said.

I nodded. "I'll run it by corporate, but I don't think they'll have any problems with it."

"Dear, and you solved the case. Go you!" Mrs. Canterbury said, pumping a fist in the air.

I was really happy with myself. "All right, Mrs. Canterbury, thanks for stopping by, and thanks for the apple cider. I'll see you around."

The next thing I did was turn on the Bose sound system and make a very important announcement: "Dear Parkstone residents, good news! The murder mystery has been solved, the culprit is caught, and life in the building is getting back to normal. Enjoy your day however you'd like, without the worries of yesterday. The team at Baxter Enterprises and your friendly concierge thank you for your patience."

I clicked it off, and smiled.

Next step was to call Royce Baxter at Baxter Enterprises and tell him the murderer had been caught and that I helped lead them to her. I also needed to make sure I got my job back. I called Royce's blackberry number to reach him directly. I heard him fumble with his cellphone before answering.

"Hi, Cassie, I have an important meeting in ten minutes," he said.

"I promise this won't take up too much of your time," I said, not being able to hide my exuberance. "They found her."

"Who's missing?" he said. "I don't have a lot of time here, Cassie. You'll have to be more specific."

"The murderer!"

There was a pause before he said, "Well, that's the best news I've heard in 24 hours. Who's the culprit?"

"Bunny Ace killed Kip," I said, sad again just thinking about it.

"You're kidding me?" he said. His tone was one of complete astonishment. "I can't believe it. No way in a million years would I have ever thought Bunny was capable of harming anyone, let alone her husband."

"Believe it," I said. "The detectives have her in handcuffs now and are taking her to the station in a police car."

"Well, I'm glad this case is finally resolved," he said. "And thank you for communicating all of the case updates."

"And I helped put the pieces together to find out she was the murderer," I said. I was hoping this declaration would help in my re-hiring process.

"Cassie, not to worry," he said. "If you'd like to continue your job as Parkstone's daytime concierge, we'd love to have you."

On the inside I was dancing with happiness, but tried to keep my composure for Royce. "I'd love to, sir," I said, so relieved.

A couple minutes later, Royce said goodbye, and I thought of other loose ends that may need tying up, now that I was permanently back to being the Parkstone concierge.

I didn't want to worry Royce about Mr. Gillrot locking me in the wine cellar, but I would bring it up with Eric again later and make sure he would take steps to ensure the curmudgeon got what he deserved. He was a resident so I didn't want to wish him ill, but he did trap me in a wine cellar with no regard to how I was going to get out.

I sighed thinking about Eric and about how our date night would finally happen, and the only thing arresting would be my short, form-fitting red dress that I'd saved for a special occasion.

Then I filled up Jet-Setter and Cashmere's food bowl. I fixed my off-kilter name placard, so "Cassie Hall, Concierge," faced directly forward. My eye caught the Parkstone brochure that Kip had signed for me the day he and Bunny moved in. I propped it up next to my name placard, so his phrase—*Stay out of life's bunkers*—was prominently displayed.

Then I took the keys from off the desk and I walked toward the courtyard's double doors. It was time to do building rounds, and I was going to be sure to make them on time. I headed out to the courtyard with my mug of cider, something to sip during my walk.

THE END

ALL ABOUT THE AUTHOR

Sherry Lodge has been writing for more than a decade for both print and online. She's written for local newspapers in both Massachusetts and Washington, D.C., where she currently writes and edits web material for a major non-profit organization.

In addition to writing, Sherry loves to watch golf, which inspired Kip Ace as one of the main characters in her debut novel, *Courtyard Corpse*. Sherry has a master's degree in journalism from Boston University.